BEHIND CLC DOORS

An anthology of work by Eastwood Writers (Glasgow)

Printed January 2021 by Amazon
Compiled and Edited by Pamela Duncan
Assistant Editors - Gerry and Joyce McKendry
and Emily M Clark

Cover designed by Andrew Skinner

ISBN 9798586298997

ACKNOWLEDGEMENTS
Eastwood Writers Production Team
acknowledges the technological advice of Gerry
Mann, Sophie Duncan and Sheila and
Andrew Skinner

Every book sold will generate a £1 donation to
Macmillan Cancer Care

CONTENTS PAGE

THE SPEARMINT CHEWING GUM AND THE MACAROON BAR

By Donald Montgomery

"It's a shame, so it is, he never gets any visitors."
"Right enough, but gie him his due, he's no any trouble. Quite happy in his ain wee world."
The two carers exchanged views, talking about the old man as through he was as inanimate as the wheelchair they were manoeuvring onto the terrace.
"There y'are, the fresh air'll do you the world of good.'
'Blow away the cobwebs, so it will."
Having settled the old man in a shaded spot, the two nurses toddled off, steeling themselves to deal with less amenable residents.
The old man sighed contentedly, closed his eyes and savoured the warmth of the August afternoon. Totally relaxed, he abandoned himself to the blessed release of reverie, in his mind, he meandered down the trails of fond recall, to a time when his weary bones were young.
Suspended in that blissful state of timelessness he heard again the vendor's cry.
'Get yer Spearmint Chewing Gum and the Macaroon Bar!'
The once familiar call echoed down the years. Shouted by gallous street traders, eager to make a bob or two from ration-starved spectators, flocking to football matches in the drab post-war days.
The long-forgotten cry, took him back to a Saturday afternoon of his boyhood days, the first day of the new football season.

The boy came off the Number Five tramcar with his father and crossed the busy Cathcart Road, to join the wave of happy souls surging towards the turnstiles at Cathkin Park, stoor rising from the dry cinders beneath their feet.

The hot August sun beat down on the diehard fans. Gap-toothed men in shabby de-mob suits. Older men, dressed sternly in three-piece outfits, watch fobs slung importantly across their waistcoats and, despite the heat, ubiquitous flat tweed bunnets.

Adding a touch of colour to the scene were wives and girlfriends in bright print dresses. Showy spivs with pencil thin moustaches and nicotine- stained fingers mingled with grubby artisans in working clothes. Red-faced men who'd enjoyed a fly pint before the pubs closed at half past two, betrayed by their boozy breath. Amid the throng, recently conscripted youths, heads cruelly shorn, mixed deferentially with veterans of two world wars.

The boy, like many another, wore his usual summer garb; short sleeved shirt and khaki shorts, held up with a two-toned snake belt.

As they neared the turnstiles the mass of bodies amazingly compacted into orderly lines, accosted now by other vendors, lackeys of the club.

'Oo-fis h-al Programme!' they bawled, and raked in the tanners.

At the cranky turnstile his father lifted him over, much to the chagrin of a clutch of urchins, begging someone   -- anyone -- to; 'Gie's a lift ower, mister!'

Once inside, they made their way round the foot of the terrace banked behind the goal.

To their left the infamous grandstand, nicknamed The Cowshed for obvious reasons, ran along one side of the pitch. But his father preferred the more immediate view from the high terrace opposite the stand.

This popular terrace sloped upward forever, or at least as far as Prospecthill Road. Not that any but the most intrepid or longsighted would choose to climb that far.

The lower reaches were stepped with rotting railway timbers and dotted with stout barriers to prevent crushing. Perversely the barriers were more popularly used as leaning posts, each one zealously guarded by their Saturday regulars, membership as exclusive as a Pall Mall club.

Wafting now and then, came a whiff of pungent pipe-smoke and relayed through loudspeakers, a jaunty Jimmy Shand record, played at irregular speeds on an unreliable gramophone.

Looking out, the view of the pitch was breath taking. The boy had been told often enough the playing surface at Cathkin Park was better than any other in the country. And on the first day of the new season, who could deny it. The green sward looked as smooth as a bowling green, and after the respite of the close season even the goalmouths were as lush and unmarked as the rest of the area. The stout goalposts, newly painted, stood out dramatically white, the scene set for the drama to come.

Approaching three o'clock all eyes focused on the quaint wee house, standing incongruously to the right of The Cowshed as viewed from the popular terrace.

The offices and the dressing rooms were situated in this corner of the ground, and it was from here the teams would emerge to kick off the long-awaited new season.

'C'mon the HiHi!' roared the crowd as the players ran out. This was the war cry of the regiment from whom the club took its name; the Third Lanark Rifles.

The boy joined in the acclaim, excited by the first sight of the scarlet jerseys and of his heroes, among them the great Jimmy Mason, and taking his place between the posts, wee Jocky Robertson, the smallest goalkeeper in Scotland.

Although Jimmy Mason was his favourite, he was equally intrigued by the full-back, Balunas. Mostly on account of his comical sounding name and the obvious derision it inspired. The player nevertheless had an important role in the side. It was a brave man who went into the tackle with Matt Balunas and his Clyde-built boots.

Even at the start of a new season there was no great expectation that the team would do any better this year than in previous seasons. Supporting Third Lanark was a way of life, not a path to glory. Success for Thirds and their supporters would mean a mid-table finish in the League and a decent cup run. Victories against Clyde and Queen's Park, their nearest neighbours would be expected and the occasional triumph against either Rangers or Celtic would provide the icing on the cake.

As play got under way the action on the field was fast and furious. The reaction from the terrace reflected the ebb and flow of the game, punctuated with witty quips and rancorous advice.

Too young to understand much of the comment and not yet versed in the finer points of the game, the boy nevertheless added his youthful voice to the commotion, urging the men in scarlet to prevail.

And prevail they did. Late in the game Thirds scored the winning goal, provoking a deafening roar. Thrilled by the intensity of the jubilant eruption the boy joined in, leaping and shouting, joy unconfined, loving the insanity of the moment.

At the final whistle he stayed close to his father, lest he got lost in the crush of bodies making for the exits.

An almost perfect day; he'd been back to Cathkin to see the Thirds and the HiHi had won. The memory had been so real the old man thought he was homeward bound on a shoogly old tramcar, before he realised it was only the carers making heavy work of moving his wheelchair back indoors.

Later that night as he drifted contentedly to sleep, the details of his daydream faded but his heart retained a warm nostalgic glow. He consoled himself with the thought that though he may not have any visitors, he was blessed with a priceless trove of memories. Happy to live his life over again, he dozed off. Tomorrow would be another yesterday.

****

HOMESICK

By Anjana Sen

"Are you homesick?" she asks, every time I call.
"No, I'm not," I say, "not homesick at all."
This here is my home since our baby was small
Her life measured in inches on my bright kitchen wall.
"There's really not much to miss," I say
Apart from you, Ma, who live so far away.
We have the telephone though, we talk every day
And it's here in Glasgow I choose to stay.
Where folk are friendly and full of cheer,
Needing fish 'n chips with lots of beer.
The only thing I don't like here
Is the dratted rain all 'round the year.
"Are you homesick?" they ask if I'm deep in thought.
"I'm not homesick," I reply, truly I'm not.
This here is my home, this house we bought
In the land we love, where we've cast our lot
With the Lochs, the Ochs, the Bonnie Lasses,
The Glens, the Hens, the Irn Bru glasses.
The football matches with heaving masses,
The Christmas presents with concert passes.
People in queues always up for a chat.
In buses and trains, we chew the fat
About the weather, the world, the neighbour's cat.
And strangers become friends, just like that.

"Am I homesick?" I ask myself, once I'm alone with me
When winter evenings don't know what-o'clock to be.
I'm not sure, I whisper, but I do yearn to see
Bougainvillaea bushes and a ripe mango tree.
Wall-to-wall sunshine ten months around
Then smell the monsoon as it thunders down
On parched earth, all cracked and brown.
But these longings, I quickly drown
As I think of the love, I have in my heart
For my forever-home, where I work on my art.
My two worlds may be oceans apart
But I'm never homesick, as I've said from the start.

****

ATTITUDES

By Pamela Duncan

Negativity negates,
Positivity creates.
Tune into the positive,
switch off the negative,
And find inspiration.

****

LUCKY CHAP?

By Gerry McKendry

Sitting in my car
outside the sports centre
A brand new BMW
Convertible
Lucky Bugger

He's got no worries I thought
No debts
No overdraft
No mortgage
And good-looking too
Lucky Bugger

No problem getting the girls
No problem wining and dining them
Look at that hair
Taylor Ferguson
and the suit is Armani
Lucky Bugger

And then he smiled at me
Perfect teeth
He beckoned me
Passenger window purred down
All leather interior
Lucky Bugger

And then he spoke
Cultured voice
Sorry to trouble you
Can you help with my wheelchair?
You see, he said still smiling
I've got no legs.

****

THE SUNWORSHIPER

By Donald Montgomery

On her first day in Spain
She lay out in the sun
For a tan to show off
Upon her return.
She took a book of poems
Intending to read them by turns.
She started with Browning
But she ended with Burns.

****

HAPPY AS LARRY

By Alistair MacLellan

Liz was wakened by loud off-key singing from the bathroom where Larry, her husband, was showering. She was annoyed at the disturbance, and shouted, "Stop pretending that you are Caruso."

"Caruso is dead, ya daft wee woman."

"That's exactly what you sound like, a dead singer."

"If it wasn't for the fact that I am a gentleman, I'd pull you in here fully dressed."

"So, there's a gentleman in our shower? In that case, where are you Larry?"

He couldn't help but laugh. Thoroughly pleased at her minor victory, Liz gladly went into the kitchen to organise their breakfast. After they had chatted and eaten, Larry went off to work in high spirits, especially since it was Friday, the end of the working week. Liz tidied up, then fixed up her shopping list, and went off to the supermarket. The rest of the day passed without incident, and, in the late afternoon, she enjoyed a mug of tea, and read her favourite magazine, The People's Friend, as she waited for Larry to come home.

Her peace and quiet was suddenly, and loudly disturbed, by the front door being barged open and Larry announcing, "All's well, Turtle Dove, your Sir Overalls has returned to his castle, and to his dream of a wife."

She loved how he always could make her feel good about herself. She and Larry were far from well-off, but by carefully budgeting, they were able to enjoy a reasonable social life. They very much looked forward to going to The Tudor Cinema on the edge of town once a month or so, when there was money in the purse.

"What's the Blue-Ribbon Chef presenting this evening?" was Larry's genial question.

"Irish Stew, swede mash, followed by a slice of apple pie."

"A feast, indeed, my lady. As usual, I congratulate you, and do so with gratitude. However, I'll need to watch my weight. Big Willie Cooper next door has put on three stone in no time at all."

"For goodness sake," she reminded him, "the only exercise he gets is going to Giovanni's chippy each night." They had a good laugh together. The atmosphere was a homely quiet in 23 Glebe as they did justice to the meal.

Leaving the table, Larry was moved to tell her, "As always, thank you Liz."

He bent down to kiss her brow. The sparkle in her eyes demonstrated how much she valued his words.

"Right then," Larry announced. "I'll go and get dressed for the Golf Club's Players of the Year celebration. Being one of the winners is amazing. I still can't believe it! I can't imagine it will ever sink in!" Beaming he headed up the stairs.

Seconds later, the stillness was broken with a roar, "Where's my suit?" A very much annoyed Larry exploded into the room.

Liz's heart hammered, and near to tears, she whispered, "Oh Larry, I am so, so sorry, I forgot about your big night. I had to pay that huge bill from the Council. I had avoided doing so since we were a bit short of money, and they sent a "final demand", with a drastic warning of the consequences if we didn't pay up immediately. In desperation I pawned your good suit and the few pieces of jewellery that I have. Fortunately, it was just enough to settle the bill."

"Look, I understand," he gently reassured her, "but I can't go the ceremony in my working clothes. I hope you can see that."

"I honestly do." She paused for a moment or two, and then she smiled, as if she had seen a light which had revealed to her a possible solution to the problem. Tentatively, indeed, but none the less hopefully determined, she suggested that they should go together next door to wee Annie, as she was called.

Larry, looked rather confused, but wanting to avoid causing her hurt, listened carefully to her idea.

Liz then reminded him that Annie's brother Tommy had never married, and had lived with her for many a year. Sadly, only eight years ago, he had unexpectedly died. In her grief, Liz explained, the wee soul couldn't bring herself to get rid of his clothes. "As if it was a brainwave, I suddenly remembered that he had been in the Salvation Army. You are about the same size as he was. Maybe the suit's still there and you could borrow it? Come on, we'll go and knock her door."

"Thank you, thank you, Liz, you are an angel in disguise right enough," was his enthusiastic reply as they left the room and knocked on their neighbour's door.

"Come away in," Annie invited them both, "it's always good to have a wee blether with you. Truly, you are more friends than just neighbours."

Annie carefully listened as Liz told her about the problem. "Of course, you can have whatever you need that suits you," was her enthusiastic response. "The clothes are still in the cupboard in Tommy's bedroom. let's nip upstairs and rummage around to see what's there." Up they went.

"Oh, Annie," Liz remarked as she looked round the room, "I really like how your wallpaper works so well with your curtains. You certainly have good taste."

She was about to add to her congratulations, when Larry gave her a dig in her side and accompanied it with a forced cough. She took the hint and kept quiet.

Annie opened the cupboard door and stood aside to let them see inside. The clothes were obviously well looked after. Annie reached in and removed the Salvation Army suit which was covered by a plastic bag, and hung it on the door knob.

However, before she removed the cover, she warned them that the suit had been undisturbed for all the years since her Tommy had died. She didn't expect it to be in top condition. Added to that, she told them, he had loved the work which he did, and so had worn the uniform a lot.

"I understand," Larry reassured her, "Thank you for telling me. I'm just fair delighted to be given such a really smart suit. That's what matters most."

Annie beamed with pride. "I know that Tommy, if he was here, would have been really pleased to help solve someone's problems. That's what he was like," she added, as she quietly dabbed her eyes with a tissue. "Right then, that's enough of that," she firmly declared. "It's back to business. You will need to try it on for size." With a cheeky grin, she smiled at Liz as she suggested that he should go into the next room to change rather than to do so in front of her.

In next to no time he returned, pleased beyond belief since the suit fitted him perfectly. He reached out and hugged Annie. "Honestly, I don't know how to thank you," he said with a lump in his throat.

"Wait a minute, Mr Style," Liz challenged him. "What about a hug for me?" A wee bit embarrassed, he wholeheartedly responded, and they all shared a right good laugh.

Annie suggested that of the three of them, she was the happiest. "You see," she explained, "I know that up there in his wee nook in heaven, Tommy's doing the Highland fling for what I've done tonight. So, be on your way then and take care."

As they left together, Larry, filled with emotion, couldn't speak, so Liz expressed their joy and gratitude with a massive hug and kiss. Annie, feeling truly humbled and satisfied with her Tommy- motivated generosity, shut the door. Then, just as she had done in similar happy circumstances as an excited wee girl, she had a wee skip on her way back to the kitchen. Unfortunately, her age caught up with her, and she stumbled onto the floor. On her bottom, shaken but unhurt, she ruefully muttered, "Bloody arthritis."

In high spirits, they took off for the club, with Larry much less bothered by the fact that he was wearing a uniform. It was a suit, that's what mattered he told himself. Filled with the renewed confidence which this gave him, and with Liz proudly sharing it, they made their way to the function suite where the ceremonies to honour the various winners of the club's annual competitions were to be recognised and rewarded. On entering the grand hall, they were most appreciative of the warmth of the people gaily greeting them.

However, the back-slapping and congratulation hugs was to take its toll on the old jacket.

On seeing the sartorial elegance of the other prize-winners, Larry had, at first, felt rather undressed. However, filled with the spirit of a people who had endured hardship in their lives, he dismissed the negative doubts about his worthiness to be present there. He was a good upstanding man. That's what mattered.

To their pure delight, and worthy pride, he was eventually announced as the winner of the Principal Poker event of the year. When he went up to the stage to receive his trophy, as he reached out to accept it, to his horror, the right sleeve of his ancient jacket fell off! Though surprised, and wholly amused, the audience first laughed loud and long.

Then, quick to appreciate the drama which seriously affected Larry, they generously quietened down. Jim, the Master of Ceremonies for the evening, quickly saved the day when he announced that Larry was jokingly reassuring anyone who might have thought he had cheated to win by having something up his sleeve.

A greatly relieved Larry, was presented with the trophy. He stood still for a moment as he paraded it before the audience in the approved manner of winners then exited the stage, acknowledging the applause. But the look he gave Liz warned her to make sure that there was to be no repeat of her forgetfulness. Her response to it was the reassurance he most needed. Much too soon, the evening drew to a close, and Larry went to reclaim his Salvation Army cap which he had left in the cloakroom. He was astonished to find it filled with money. Very surprised, and totally unsure about what to do with it, he took comfort and remained confident that Liz would know what to do about it.

He was greatly relieved when they got home out of the pouring rain.

Without even taking off his soaking clothes, he asked, "Ok, my lady, what should I do with the money? I'm afraid that I might be accused of stealing it if I keep it, though we could solve a few problems with it? I need your wise counsel."

She smiled at the compliment as she popped into the kitchen. "I'll make a cup of tea first, and then decide what to do. My mother always used to say, 'there's never a problem after enjoying a wee cup of tea'. Let me think about it while I make it."

Even before the kettle had boiled, she came out of the kitchen and, sitting beside Larry on the couch, she proposed that they should give the money to wee Annie whose finances were rather meagre.

Not that Annie had told anyone about that, although it was fairly obvious to all the neighbours who admired her ability to make ends meet. Indeed, the only time they heard her complain was when she told them that her newspaper had gone up by three pence. "Right then, my knight in shining armour, let's do it". With a daft big grin on his face he joined her, and together they went out and knocked her door.

Annie was dumbfounded when they gave her the money and explained the background to the gift. Then, with a tear in her eye, and a beautiful smile, she offered half of the money to them, saying "You are in as much need as me. If you really mean to make me happy, then please accept it."

This time it was the couple who were speechless. In the spirit of a good and considerate neighbour, Larry moved to decline the offer. Liz however, recognised the worth and importance of the genuineness of Annie's gesture, and managed to quickly alert Larry to that. To her relief, he nodded his understanding of the situation.

It proved to be an occasion which was, in fact, an advantage to anyone who was prepared to come out of their comfort zone and respond to a need which they knew was in their power to address. Above all, it's good, and uplifting, when people clearly understand that kindness and generosity have the power to be contagious.

****

HOGMANAY

By Ann Morrison

It was Daisy and Joe's second Hogmanay. Last year due to Daisy being heavily pregnant, had been a quiet affair. 1956 was going to be different. The young couple had gone to a great deal of trouble making sure everything was exactly right in their modest little semi on the outskirts of Glasgow. It is an almost forgotten fact that Christmas was not designated a public holiday in Scotland until 1958. Before then, New Year was the big celebration. On Hogmanay houses would be cleaned, a steak pie prepared ready for the oven, and shortbread and black bun laid out on the sideboard along with the Ne'erday bottle. Families would gather together waiting for 'the bells', ready to welcome first-footers on the stroke of midnight. Hopefully the first over the threshold would be a tall dark handsome man, with a lump of coal to place on the fire while saying "Lang may yer lum reek."

Both sets of parents were coming to bring in the New Year. Daisy had been up since dawn with the baby, and by midday every surface in the house shone. She was proud as she looked round her cosy little sitting room. The windows sparkled, the rugs were vacuumed, the floor surround had been polished and a warm fire was burning merrily in the grate. The gleaming mirror above the fireplace reflected the sideboard, resplendent with Daisy's precious wedding china all set out ready for visitors.

There was a knock at the door. It was Bill their next-door neighbour.

"Daisy, Joe, do you fancy coming through for a cup of tea – or maybe something stronger?"

"Tea would be great, Bill," Joe replied with a smile. "I think we'd better keep the something stronger for later. Mind you if Daisy doesn't stop polishing, there'll be no furniture left when the family arrive."

"It's your mum, Joe, she's always so perfect and …"

"Daisy, Mum's had twenty-five years to learn to be perfect. Thanks, Bill, we'll be with you in a minute."

"Oh, give me half-an-hour, will you? I can't get the blinking fire to draw. Once I get it going and the room's warmed up, I'll give you a shout. It's a right cold day and we don't want the wee one to get chilled."

Bill was a decent enough old chap, a lonely bachelor who delighted in having the young couple as neighbours. What is more, he doted on the baby. Trouble was he was not all that bright and had the unfortunate habit of frequently making decisions that inevitably got him embroiled in trouble.

Little did Daisy and Joe guess, as they proudly gazed at their little daughter sleeping peacefully in her pram in the corner of her mother's immaculate sitting room, that they were about to be caught up in one of Bill's misadventures.

Bill tried repeatedly to get his fire to catch, but with no success. Time was going on and Daisy and Joe would soon be through for their promised cup of tea. He had to get the room warmed up.

"Oh, to hang with it," he muttered, rummaging under the kitchen sink and bringing out a rusty old can of paraffin. Soaking a piece of rag in the highly flammable liquid, he laid it on top of the coals.

One match was all it took. The flames caught the loose soot in the chimney and, with a roar like a rocket going off, they leapt up into the frosty sky.

"What the …?" Joe shouted as he ran outside to see what caused the noise. "Bill, your chimney's on fire," he yelled. "It's a bad one, mate. Quick dial 999 and call the fire brigade."

In no time at all, to the delight of the neighbourhood children who gathered to watch, firemen were scrambling over the roof putting their hoses down the chimney. Problem was, due to all the smoke, they went down the wrong chimney, and Daisy's perfect house was engulfed in soot and dirty water. Every surface she had lovingly cleaned and polished was smeared with the filthy stuff. It was when she saw the baby with soot all over her little face that the poor girl burst into tears.

Joe ran out to tell the firemen their mistake.

"I'm so sorry," one of them said, coming in to survey the damage. "Don't you worry, it's our fault and we'll clean it all up."

And clean it up they did. Once the fire was out in Bill's chimney and the loft had been checked for any smouldering, the firemen set to and removed every bit of dirt from Daisy's house, except for the soot on the wedding china, she didn't trust them with that.

Poor Bill was distraught when he came to apologise. Daisy sat him down and his young neighbours kindly assured him that it was all just an unfortunate accident. The main thing was that nobody had been hurt. The old man was so upset Joe took pity on him and opened his Ne'erday bottle. After a dram, Bill took himself back next door and Daisy and Joe were able to take stock of what had happened.

Later that night the chimney fire was the story of the day, if not of the year. Joe's mum said she was impressed how well Daisy had coped. Daisy's dad said some very rude things about Bill but, in the end, everyone agreed no harm had been done.

At midnight, when the bells rang out and all the ships in the river blew their horns to welcome in the New Year, Daisy and Joe had their first foot. He was not particularly tall, and a bit past being handsome, but at least he did bring a bit of coal with him.

"Lang may yer ...," Bill started to say as he made to drop the lump of coal on the fire.

"Don't," Joe laughingly interrupted before handing their neighbour a glass. "There's been enough reekin' round here for one day!"

"Well I want you all to know there'll be no more fires in my house," Bill announced, sipping his whisky. "I see the Co-Op are offering a great wee coal effect electric fire in their January sale. I intend to be first in the queue when they open."

Joe's mother gave Bill a great big hug and Daisy's father poured him another glass.

"Happy New Year," they all said in unison.

****

MANGOES

by *Ashima Srivastava*

It was the end of May and the sun was beating down on a hot Thursday afternoon. Sita's grandmother was calling out to her to come in for her lunch. She had been out playing hopscotch with her friends. It was the school summer holidays and Sita's parents had dropped her off at her maternal grandparents' house on their way to work and would pick her up on their way back. Sita sat down for her favourite lunch of hot buttered chapatis with sweet juicy mangoes and an ice-cold lassi.

The monsoons had arrived early in Mumbai and this was the last of the Alphonso mangoes (king of mangoes) that Sita would eat for this year. Her grandmother knew how much she loved them and would make sure Sita had them every day while they were available. As soon as she had finished eating, she wanted to go out to play but her grandfather told her it was too hot to go outside and that she should take a nap.

"Only if you tell me a story Nana (grandfather)," she said. She lay in her grandfather's lap and he started his story, but it wasn't the story her grandmother told her every afternoon. Sita told her grandfather she wanted to hear the bad man story. Her grandfather said he didn't know that one but the one he was telling her had the circus with clowns, lions, elephants and that she should close her eyes and listen. Sita was having none of that and jumping up from his lap went to look for her Nani (grandmother).

On finding her she said, "Nani hurry up, it's story time." Her grandmother told her to go lie down and that she would tell her the story once she had finished tidying up.

The little girl waited impatiently under cool sheets with the fan humming in the background. She could feel her eyelids getting heavy but was fighting hard to stay awake. After what seemed like an eternity but was no more than a few minutes her grandmother came and lay down beside her. Sita immediately snuggled up to her grandmother all wide awake and excited to hear her favourite story. Nani started patting her on her back. Shutting her eyes, Sita waited for her grandmothers' soothing voice to flow over her.

The story is called Mangoes her grandmother said as she began narrating it in an affectionate tone. 'Once upon a time, very long ago in a land called Pavitra (meaning pure), there was a powerful and honest king, who with his wife ruled his subjects with generosity and a kind heart. Everyone in his kingdom was happy and there was no crime.'

Even though she had heard the story many times, Sita's curiosity and questions stretched to extract every precious moment out of the story until she drifted off to sleep. It was almost a game between the two, Nani could predict when the next question was coming and she would pause expectantly for the interruptions. 'The king and his wife had a beautiful daughter called Malini.'

Kissing her on her forehead her grandmother said, 'The princess was as beautiful as you are Sita,' this always made Sita smile and she hugged her grandmother even tighter. Continuing with the story Nani said Malini would start her morning by offering prayers in the temple and then studying. Her afternoons were filled with learning music, painting, archery, governance and warfare. She was an only child and doted on by her parents. Malini had a sweet voice and every time she sang, it brought joy to everyone who heard her. She had often been told she sang like a Koel (a small blackbird from the same family as a Cuckoo).

'One day a merchant came from a land far away with his carts full of grains, silks, sarees, toys and tricks and set up shop around the corner from the temple that Malini prayed at every day. Business was good and he stayed in the kingdom for a few days flogging his wares during the day and strolling around the town taking in the sights in his free time.

One evening he stopped dead in his tracks at the sound of a soft melodious voice. Drawn towards it as though in a trance he found himself at the entrance of the palace asking the guards if they knew who was singing so beautifully. They replied with a smile and took immense pride in saying it was their princess practising her singing.

The merchant wanting to know more asked 'When will she be practising again? How long does she practice for?' He was told that she very diligently practised every afternoon at the same time. He was so enchanted by the voice that he couldn't wait to hear her sing again. The rest of the day passed very slowly.

The following afternoon he was once again captivated by her voice. He thought of how nice it would be to come home to that sweet voice every day. The merchant had beautifully embroidered sarees and silks and wanted to exhibit them for the queen. It was there that he met Malini and showed her a few magic tricks and pretended to befriend her. Malini was very keen to learn magic tricks and the merchant started teaching her.

A few days later he convinced Malini to go to the inn he was staying in so that he could show her one last magic trick before he left. Malini went with him but her trust was betrayed when she was snatched and hidden away in a chest. The merchant left for his town and with him was the princess concealed in one of the many carts.

On reaching home, he made sure Malini was confined to a single room, she was looked after very well, but was no longer free. The merchant would ask her to sing for him when he came back from his trips.

As the days passed the gilded cage sapped all the joy out of Malini's singing. Instead of happiness in her voice when she sang, now you could feel the pain of betrayal and sorrow. Days turned into weeks and then into months before the merchant allowed her to finally step out of the house.

He had fallen ill and could no longer go out to sell his wares and was compelled to ask Malini to go from street to street selling toys and magic tricks. Malini went out every morning and returned in the evening with most of the goods sold. She went from street to street singing and even though she was sad inside, her voice would still draw both the young and old out of their homes to hear that beautiful voice.

Every day Malini went further and further to sell the toys. One day, as she was walking down the street singing, a door burst open to her left and an old man came stumbling out towards her, his arms flailing as he pointed repeatedly to her and the heavens, his lips were moving furiously without making any sounds.

It was a voice he would have known anywhere. Even though Malini wasn't dressed like a princess he knew it was her and he lurched his way up to her.

As soon as Malini saw him, she burst into tears. It was her music teacher. He took her indoors to his family and they fed Malini and gave her a clean set of clothes to wear after she had washed. The very next morning they sat in their bullock carts and headed towards Pavitra. The sparkle had come back to Malini's eyes. She was smiling and laughing again.

The merchant though unwell had gone out looking for Malini when she didn't come back in the evening. He had searched for her late into the night but had returned home despondent at not having found her.

News that Malini had been found and was coming home had reached the palace. Her parents couldn't stop crying when they saw Malini run up the stairs and into their arms.

That evening there was a big celebration and offerings of Alphonso Mangoes were made to god to thank him for bringing Malini back home. She settled into her old life, always thankful to her teacher who had brought her back. Nani finished the story and looked down to see Sita fast asleep with a smile on her face.

As she tried to extract herself from Sita's arms, the girl woke up and hearing the pitter-patter of rain was too excited to go back to sleep. It was the first rain of the season and the unmistakable smell of the parched earth soaking up the rain drifted to her.

The Mumbai monsoons are a force of nature. It can rain continuously for days leading to flooding and chaos, but despite that life doesn't come to a standstill. Sita asked her grandmother if they would still be able to go to the market. Her grandmother said yes, and they set out when there was a break in the showers.

Sita could see the man at the corner of the road on his cart roasting corn on the cob on a small fire pit, she could smell the samosas being fried by the roadside and the aroma of the Bombay sandwich being toasted in a small roadside kiosk.

On the way, they stopped at the temple to offer flowers and prasad and fed hay to the cow tied to the side of the temple.

As they started to make their way back home the skies opened and the colours of the rainbow flooded the pavements_as umbrellas of all shapes and sizes flew open making walking on the pavements as tricky as trying to avoid the numerous potholes and splashes from vehicles going past. Once back and dry with the air conditioner at full blast, the outside heat, humidity and car horns were all quickly forgotten.

As she stood waiting on the balcony for her parents, she looked out at the sea which surrounded her grandparents' flat on three sides.

The view from here was so different from the one in her parents' flat. Sita felt the cool breeze on her face and the smell of drying fish wafted up. She looked at the fishing boats setting out into the vastness of the sea and thought how similar they looked to the paper boats she would try to sail in the puddles.

As the rain stopped Sita saw her parents parking the car. They looked up and waved at her as they got out. Sita was excited at seeing them and ran to tell her grandmother to open the door. Hopping from foot to foot, Sita excitedly started telling her mum how she had spent her day, all the fun she had had, the delicious mango that she had eaten and how they had got caught in the rain.

Later that night kissing her grandparents goodbye Sita said she would see them tomorrow. As she walked down the stairs with her mum, she saw her grandmother standing at the door with love brimming in her eyes and a smile on her face.'

****

HINDSIGHT

By Donald Montgomery

The understanding came belated.
After he had been castrated.
Sadly now he realised
He only wanted circumcised.

****

DEATH BE NOT PROUD

By Anjana Sen

She stirs in her sleep. Something disturbs her usual deep slumber, aided by the low dose of sleeping pills her GP insists on.

"It's time to go," whispers this breezy unknown voice, "come on, it's time to go."

"Who's there?" she calls out, scrambling to switch her bedside lamp on. "Who is it?"

Fearing the worst, (only last month, Mrs Linn in flat 2G, had a break in, she still talks about it), she sits up in bed, sleepy eyes now adjusted to the light in the room. There, sitting in her rocking chair, was the strangest man she had ever seen. No one she knew, and she knew most people in the Asian community in Glasgow. Why, she was a regular every Sunday at the Hindu temple, and hardly ever missed any function.

This person was a stranger, in the most peculiar costume she had seen. She ought to be scared, she found herself thinking. He could be a drug-taking lunatic you read about all the time. But he had such a kind smile, underneath his fearsome Viking hat and silken Indian robes, she found herself smiling back.

"How did you get in?" she asked "Did I leave the front door open again?"

"I've come to get you," he answered. "Your time has come. You need to come with me."

"My time? Who **are** you?"

"You don't recognise me? I am Yama Raja, the God of Death, and it's your time to travel back to heaven with me."

"I'm going nowhere, Mr Raj, there is nothing wrong with me. If you are a God, you should know that I am the most able member of my Yoga group. Even women in their sixties and seventies are not as good as I am. And I have never used the wheelchair service at airports, even though my sons want me to."

She gets out of bed, puts on her robe and goes into the sitting room, beckoning him to follow.

"Young man, it's rude to enter a lady's bedroom like this, don't you know?"

"Young? I'm only a few thousand years old," he mutters, but follows her into the lounge and sits where she points.

"Now, that you have woken me up, I'm going to have some tea. Would you like some?"

Without waiting for his reply, she goes into her kitchen, and fusses about with the tea things, emerging a few minutes later with a tray of tea, biscuits, and two slices of birthday cake. It was her birthday that day, well, the day before she realises, as it was past midnight. And her entire family were to have come to celebrate. Both her sons, their wives, her three grandchildren. Even her daughter was going to fly in from Oxford, to help Ma turn eighty. But, as usual, something had cropped up in each of their lives.

A broken wrist in one home, a last-minute client meeting in another and a cancelled flight in Rita's case. She was used to it. Used to their lives being more important than hers, and she knew they would come sooner or later.

They loved her; they just did not think she needed them as much as she did. But there was all this food she had cooked, and it would be such a shame to have it go to waste.

Watching this nice Mr Raj gobble down both slices of cake, an idea comes into her head. She knows how she can delay her travels with him.

"I know it's quite late, but would you like something to eat? I can heat something up quite easily."

His shocked pleasure was all the answer she needed.

"In my line of business, in all the years I have been doing this, nobody has ever offered me anything. Either they are in too much of a hurry to come with me, or I have to drag them kicking and screaming," he said.

"Well, you just put your feet up and relax now, I'll sort something out soon."

She leaves him, delighted to have someone to fuss over after such a long time. As she puts the biryani into the microwave, he comes to the kitchen with his Viking helmet in his hands, like a small errant schoolboy wanting permission from the teacher to go to the toilet.

"May I invite my friend GR to come too? I know he's in the area tonight, and he would love a plate of Indian food."

"Who's GR?" She went through the list of Hindu mythological gods in her head.

"He's my local friend, old Grimmy, we work together all the time."

"Sure," she said, "the more the merrier. But in return I want a favour too. I want to stay on till my favourite grand-daughter graduates from St Andrews next month. I've already decided what to wear; I don't want to miss that."

He agrees reluctantly and goes away to call his friend. When she lays out dinner at the dining table, which has not been used in a long while, she uses her good dinner service, cutlery and linen.

She finds herself humming, it has been so long since she hosted a dinner party. Usually her sons just took her cooking home in Tupperware containers, which their wives never returned. And the grandkids, well, they did not really like Indian food, and ate on the go at the kitchen table. As for her own friends, they preferred casual lunches these days to elaborate dinner parties. Not so easy to drive at night anymore, you see.

Looking up from her thoughts, she saw Mr Raj already seated at the table. Across from him was a very old man in a white toga like outfit, carrying an instrument she had seen farmers use to cut crops, as a child in India.

"Welcome to my home Mr Reaper," she said, after introductions had been made. "Hope you like Indian food?"

He did not look at her, or reply, but attacked his plate with the same gusto that her old Labrador used to attack her dinners.

After a very pleasant evening over dinner, more cake, sherry and green tea, it was time for the men to leave.

"We'll be back in two months," Yama Raj said.

"I'll be waiting, with a nice meal ready." she replied with a wink. "What's your favourite food?"

****

WIPEOUT

By Nada Mooney

The phone rang. It was 3am.

Tom thought it was his alarm and couldn't understand why it was still dark. When he realised it was the phone he lifted the receiver and croaked, "Hello."

A dalek-like voice shouted, "This is a warning from the Scottish Liberation Army. Your house is about to be fire bombed, so get out now. Any sign of police presence and you will be shot. We have marksmen standing by."

"You must have the wrong number," Tom gasped

"No," came the immediate reply. "Tom McKechnie. 46 Lomond Terrace. Now move it!"

Bewildered and terrified, Tom pulled a jacket over his pyjamas and fled down the stairs and out of the door. He ran as fast as his slippers would allow, with no idea where he was going until he completely ran out of breath.

Leaning against a wall he looked about trying to make sense of what had happened. Why him? It was then he noticed that the small side gate of a park was open so he slipped in and found a bench to rest on.

Sleep was out of the question. Or was he in the middle of a nightmare? No the bench was hard and a bit damp and he felt cold now that he had stopped running.

The brief message played over and over in his head – he was unaware of having upset anyone. Had he made his decision to vote NO in the referendum too widely known? Surely not? He searched for some logical answer but there was none.

The quietness of the park was frightening and reassuring at the same time. Trying to think positively, he wondered if he was insured for this strange predicament he found himself in, but would his policy go up in smoke with everything else?

So he sat, head in hands and barely noticed the birds were forming a choir and it was beginning to get light. Suddenly realising he was dressed in his pyjamas, he knew he would have to move before someone spotted him and got suspicious, so slowly and sadly he made his way back home.

As he turned into the terrace everything seemed quiet and orderly. The only person he saw was a lad delivering milk, who gave him a strange look, but said nothing.

The house seemed normal, as he cautiously pushed the door open. There was no smell of burning, but as he walked from room to room, each one was completely empty. All his possessions gone. Nothing had been overlooked, even his kettle had been taken. Not a piece of furniture remained, nothing...

Shaking violently, he reached for the phone but it was dead.

****

THE LAST SANDCASTLE

By Joyce McKendry

John stood in the doorway of the little cottage looking out over the still dark water. How can everything appear so normal, so ordinary, when nothing will ever be the same again, he thought. Looking to the right he could see faint traces of daylight beginning to appear over the top of the mountains. Another day starting as if the world could just carry on when both of their lives had ended at exactly 11.09 last night when that young doctor had uttered the dreaded words "time of death ......".

They had been sitting on the porch the night before, each with a cup of cocoa and two digestive biscuits as they watched the sun go down.

He must have dozed off slightly and when he rose he looked over at Janet - her book had slipped down over her chest and her specs were leaning haphazardly over her nose.

"Come on old girl, getting a bit nippy now. Time for bed," he'd said, stretching as he stood up, but then he'd looked more closely at Janet, and so the nightmare had begun.

Now he gently closed the door on the apparent normality that lay beyond and looked slowly round the small room that served as kitchen, sitting room and dining room in the familiar holiday cottage that had been their refuge for almost 50 years.

They had first come here when the children were small and then this cottage was the only one sitting proudly in its own little bay in this lovely corner of Cornwall.

They had been delighted to find that the water and electricity supply had newly been installed, and the children immediately announced that they were stranded in their very own desert island. They set about searching the beach and the small wood immediately behind the cottage then couldn't wait to change into swimming costumes, screams of delight coming every time the bitterly cold waves washed over them.

The sandcastles began as little mounds of sand but over the years progressed to real works of art as the children grew - Sandy's even had a moat and a drawbridge made out of twigs.

They were such happy carefree days, four of them the children, Susan and Sandy, and Janet and John – yes, they really were called Janet and John which caused much hilarity when they were introduced all those years ago - had come to the cottage for the same two weeks every year.

Gradually over time more cottages had sprung up, now there were seven in all spread around the little bay, which thankfully had retained its quiet secluded atmosphere, no yobos or blaring transistors here, just families like themselves.

Was it really almost 50 years ago that first visit? It seems like another lifetime now. He took off his coat, hung it on the hook behind the door, and filled the kettle.

As he turned, he could see daylight beginning to creep through the window but he tried to concentrate on the job in hand. He made the tea in the old brown teapot, lifted the last of the digestives, but when he turned to the table there were two cups, two saucers and two plates and he felt tears well up once again.

He couldn't face drinking the tea, so he replaced the crockery in the cupboard and busied himself with packing the suitcases into the car.

Janet always packed them the night before so they only had to add the toiletries and it was time to be off. She had brushed the floor the previous night, the sand of course, got everywhere, and she'd dusted round for the last time making sure everything was spick and span.

He looked at his watch. It was just coming up to 6 am, too early for any of the neighbours to be out and about, and in any case, he wasn't up to facing anyone with the news at the moment. He'd telephone Betty and Joe later in the day.

With a final look round, as usual he placed the keys in the basket on the little table by the door for the letting agent to collect, and knowing he would never return, with a final sigh, he whispered, "Goodbye little house, goodbye my life," Then he walked out of the door for the very last time.

****

MOUNTAIN SHADOWS

By Emily M Clark

Even in summertime i1t was cold in the shadow of Mount Monessi. Using a flask of soapy water, Tony was washing his wife's marble headstone.

"It's winter now, Maria" he told the oval photo on the headstone, "and very cold." He finished washing the stone and drained the bubbles from the flask.

"I've met a woman, Maria, very pretty and young enough to have children."

He waited as if expecting a sharp retort. The wind whistled in the trees and blasted the last of their autumn leaves onto the grave. "Yes, I knew you'd be angry. But I am lonely and I need someone."

Snow was falling as he shouldered his back-pack. "Your brother let slip about your latest. I pretended to be shocked about the *nomo* from the library"

Again, he waited for a sharp retort which came in the form of another gust of wind. "We're getting married in May. We'll both sell our flats and buy a semi in Alassio. You remember the beautiful place on the Riviera di Ponente?" He buffed the headstone with a dry cloth. "There you go; just like new." As Tony left the graveside, snow blinded him and the wind battered him. Mid-way downhill, he turned and raised his hand. "See you next month, Maria."

Like a black bony finger, a tree root caught the heel of his boot. He fell, hitting his head on a stone angel. Groaning and bleeding he lay in the swirling snow. Before he passed out, a husky voice said, " *Silenzio Antonio.* It will not be next month. I will be *un momento, mio adorato marito.*

****

BOO!

By Gerry McKendry

Another bunch of suckers, more easy money. How gullible can people be. Just change the décor in your front room, put on some gypsy clothing and watch the cash flow in.

Mystic Rosita (Helen from Barrhead) was becoming bored with the same routine. Invite a small group of women to her home, go into a trance, feed them with general statements in an affected voice. These statements are called 'Barnums' and include such specifics as "You are sometimes insecure, especially with people you don't know," and "I can see you have a box of photos or letters not sorted out."

Tonight would be different. Helen had no respect for her clients and decided she would be really dramatic just for a laugh. She told the first one that someone close to her would go to jail for murder. The second victim was told that by her actions, or inactions, a friend would die. Similar dire predictions were visited on all of tonight's customers. In fact, as the night wore on Mystic Rosita warmed to her task and began to foretell of increasingly awful futures. Naturally, the women were very upset, but, in her current mood, Helen was amused by this.

"I only tell you what the spirits tell me," she said haughtily laughing up her sleeve. She did not rise and told them to find their own way out. As the door closed behind the chattering group, Helen rose from the table but stopped in her tracks. Someone had come in when the door was still open. A man confronted her.

"You must stop misusing the spirits. Don't anger them, I warn you."
She laughed in his face, "It's all a scam, just a lark."
In a menacing voice, he said, "Are you sure?" and vanished.

****

COVID 19

By Pamela Duncan

We had such fun, but now
there is a caution in our lives
that wasn't there before.
A wariness that multiplies
To make us plead,
"Take care."

****

MY GYPSY CLARA

By Kate Richard

"It would make a good subject for a Modernist painting," John thought as he surveyed the scene, observing everything carefully as policemen are trained to do.

It was Lammas Fair in St Andrews and the main part of the town was occupied by round-abouts, Ferris wheels, stalls and their support vehicles. John had noticed a white and garish blue plastic space ship flashing its lights which threw into stark relief the crumbling black ruin behind it.

As a local historian he could not condone the mess of the Fair, but he appreciated the long traditions which led to this modern travesty. His thoughts were interrupted by his personal radio. He ran down the street, cursing the people who got in his way.

At the Shove Ha'penny stall a full-scale brawl was in progress. John had to force his way through. A swarthy man in a string vest punctuated with dark chest hairs was pummelling a weedy little man in dirty jeans and a holey sweater.

"That'll teach you to cheat, you sneaky bastard."

"I didn't mean it, guv, lay off, will you?"

As John approached, they stopped and looked warily at the officer.

"What's it all about then?" inquired John taking out his notebook.

"Nothing Officer, honestly." Replied one of the sweetest voices John had ever heard. He turned to look at the owner of the voice. Her appearance startled him. The notebook fell to the ground unnoticed. Never again, he realised would he see anyone as lovely in such unlikely circumstances. Merry brown eyes danced mischievously in a delicately formed face, framed in a mass of auburn curls.

"My brother wasn't doing anything, mister. This man was claiming a prize he never won." John could not take his eyes off her. Her dress looked washed out and skimpy but the figure underneath was alluring.

"All right now," he said to the men, "break it up, move along there." The crowd shuffled away and the stall holder retreated into the depths of his stall. John edged his way back to the girl. She seemed to have vanished completely. Suddenly he saw her peeping out from behind some shelving where the tawdry prizes were on display. She was watching him. He gave her a broad wink.

"What do you want, mister?"

"Just checking."

"We don't want trouble, just doing our business."

"I know but you lot always seem to cause bother."

The stall holder swaggered over to John. "Look here, the fight's over why don't you mind your own bloody business and get the hell out of mine?"

"O-K, I'm leaving, but there had better not be a recurrence." He stole a lingering look at the girl to which she responded with a gentle smile.

"And don't get any ideas about my sister. We don't hold with outsiders."

John had never felt like this before. He was in a daze. He wanted to protect his gypsy princess from her brutish brother and spirit her away to a secret place where no one could reach them. A small niggling doubt did enter his mind when he thought of introducing the girl to his parents. He imagined his father's comments, "Won't do your career any good, I didn't put you through the university for nothing you know."

The idea of the gypsy waif in his mother's prim sitting room where everything was immaculate brought a wry smile.

He pushed this unpleasantness to the back of his mind. How could he persuade the girl he had fallen for her before the Fair left town? It had only two days to go. Did she like him? Could he ask her for a date tonight? But she must like him. They would meet this evening. In an agony of trepidation John signed off his duty roster and a testy sergeant told him to find his notebook double quick. John ran back to the stall.

Yes, she was there. "Did you see a black notebook? I lost it in the scuffle." The girl disappeared and returned with the notebook clutched in a dirty hand. "How much is it worth?" she asked.

"A lot, now can I have it please? I'll take you out on the town tonight if you give it back."

The girl looked round furtively, her brother was nowhere to be seen.

"Yes, I'll come with you but my brother mustn't find out."

"I'll meet you at the kiddies' round-about over there about eight," said John.

The gypsy girl handed over the notebook. "Till then," she whispered.

She was there, waiting. He grabbed the girl's hand and together they dashed off on a mad whirlwind through the streets. The air throbbed with the sound of the generators whirling the machines through the sky. Heavy rock music blasted their eardrums and the smell of onions and hamburgers assaulted their nostrils. They were oblivious. The girl gazed at John as though she had never seen anyone like him before.

"What's your name?" he asked.

"Clara," she replied. "It's after me grandmother, she was a fortune-teller."

"Clara, it suits you. Have you seen the harbour? Would you like to go down there?"

"Will it take long? I can't stay out too late."

"No, it's only a little way and we can walk out along the pier." As they went past the ruins of St Mary's Church, he told her of how long ago when the harvest was gathered in and the Fair came to town, tall-masted ships would come and tie up in the harbour. As he talked the moon came out and she could see the dark shapes of the ships as they walked out onto the pier.

"Listen, John, can you hear the sailors, they are talking funny?"

"Yes, they are foreign, they come from all over the world."

"And what are they carrying in their holds?"

"Fine silks for your dresses, and fiery spices for your larder."

"What is that music coming from the bowels of the ship?"

"It is a lute and it sings only of love." As they walked further out along the pier lit by a tarry rope burning in a metal basket, they could see that some of the ships were lit by candles in lanterns. They peered into the ships' holds and saw the casks and boxes waiting to be unloaded. Smells of cinnamon and cloves wafted out from the holds. Wooden casks had black letters branded into their round sides.

"What are those letters, I'm sorry I can't read?"

"Cognac, claret, champagne, they are wines from France. Maybe they are for the King's table for perhaps the Cardinal, these idle clergy have a taste for the good things in life," answered John. "Don't worry about reading, I'll soon teach you."

Clara looked doubtful, "We can't stay long together you know, Tom expects me back."

"But we're not in Tom's time anymore, lets sail away in one of these fine ships and they'll never find us."

"How I wish we could."

"Let's go aboard this one," said John helping her down the ladder. As they passed the great wheel which steered the ship they saw 'Great Michael' engraved upon it. "This is the King's ship, it was built for him only last year."

"Should we be here?"

"Come, they are waiting for us."

As they entered the main cabin bending their heads in the narrow entranceway a servant came forward. Silently he showed them to the table where a meal was laid out. Clara had never seen so much food all at once, not even at the big Romany feasts.

"It's marvellous, how can we eat it all?"

"You don't have to eat all of it," laughed John. "Just pick what you like, taste what you fancy." He was loving her more with every passing moment.

Some of the flavours were strange but exciting and Clara tucked in heartily. After eating her fill, Clara sank happily into John's embrace as the stretched out on a long seat under the port holes. The ship rocked gently.

"I wish this could go on for ever," said John.

"It can't you know that, they'll find us, gypsies have strange powers."

"I know, I just wish, that's all," John sighed. "Come, I'll take you back."

A cold wind sprang up and the moon went behind a cloud. When Clara looked back to the sea, the ships had vanished.

"Where have they gone, will we ever see them again?"

"It was our night of magic that made them come, who knows if they'll come again?"

Passing through the gate of the eerie churchyard John took Clara into the shelter of a giant ornate tombstone. He put his arms round her and kissed her gently at first but with increasing urgency.

"Please stay here, come and live with me."

"I love you," came the wistful reply, "but I can't stay. Your family would not like me and my brother will beat me black and blue."

"Of course, my family will like you and will come to love you as much as I do. I love you so much."

"That's enough." A rough hand seized John's collar and he was wrenched out of Clara's despairing grasp. John's police training came to the fore and after a struggle he managed to free himself and to tackle his opponent. A smell of stale sweat and beer made him retch as his assailant wrestled with him.

"Can I arrest this man?" he argued with himself. "What do I tell the Sarge?" Distracted for a moment, John let the gypsy wriggle free and he ran off. Clara followed swiftly.

"Come back, come back to me," John called. "I love you, I need you."

There was no reply. John struggled to his feet and gave chase. He spotted his quarry running back towards Market Street and the Fair. His breath was coming fast there was a pain in his ribs where the gypsy had punched him but he ran on. "I must find her."

As he ran past the entrance to a vennel he could hear footsteps in the distance. He paused, yes there were two pairs and they were running. He dived into the pitch darkness of the lane, black gleaming stone houses loomed up on either side.

There was danger everywhere. A sharp pain thudded into the side of his head and he knew no more. Groggily, he felt the lump behind his ear.

"Ouch, where am I?" He remembered and a great wave of sorrow swept over him.

Then he heard footsteps He recognised her lightness. Now he could make out her lovely face, dirty and tear stained.

"Did he hurt you bad, the dirty bastard?"

"Not too bad, I'm ok."

"You know I have to leave with the Fair tomorrow."

Reluctantly John let her go and the darkness enveloped her.

The next day John was up early and hunting for the Shove ha'penny stall, but it had gone. In mounting despair, he searched all the vehicles leaving the Fair but he could not find Clara. He even stopped some on the pretext of checking their roadworthiness but it was all useless.

In later years, happily settled with a farmer's daughter John would listen to men boasting of their conquests with the ladies. But he thought, none of them had loved a little wild gypsy with whom one could go to enchanted lands.

****

THE WESTERN FRONT'S ALL QUIET NOW

(Thoughts after a visit to the Great War battlefields)

By Donald Montgomery

The Western Front's all quiet now.
Awed, reverential pilgrims
In fondly tended cemeteries
Weep silent, angry tears.

Half a generation
Smeared across the Flemish Plain
In sprawling consecrated grounds,
Dominions of the Dead.

Soldiers of The Great War lie here
Young men who'll grow not old.
Brave patriotic Tommies,
Poor sacrificial lambs.

Imagine this: In Blighty,
There'll be no welcome in the hillside.
The only girl in the world
Condemned to soldier on without her only boy.

Her sweetheart, old kit bag packed with woe
And Tipperary still a long, long way away.
His hero's home,
A block of Portland stone.

Yes, the Western Front's all quiet now
And still the poppies grow,
Where Death once spat his bullets
In France and Flanders long ago.

****

THE WRITING GROUP

By Anjana Sen

A dozen boxes on my laptop screen
Some weeks more and some weeks less.
We write and read and share and preen.
It comforts me I must confess.

****

RONNIE RIDES A RAINBOW

By Anjana Sen

Ronnie looked out of his window. There were so many rainbows. Even more than yesterday. He was trying to decide which one he liked the best. He had finished his schoolwork for the day and had to be quiet while mum was working. She was talking to people on the computer. Ronnie giggled as he thought how mummy was wearing only half her work clothes. She still had her pyjama bottoms on. She had winked at him and said, "Shh, Darling, it's our secret." It was fun being with mum all the time, but he missed his teacher and his classroom and all his friends.

He missed daddy, too. But daddy was working with very sick people and could not come home. He looked so tired and old when he called to say goodnight every night. Poor daddy. Ronnie wanted to go and play outside. He wanted to cycle up and down the street with his friend Billy, like they used to. Or play on the swings in the park. Or visit Gran and climb the big tree in her garden.

But he could not do any of that because of The Germ! Ronnie wished this Big, Bad Germ would go away. There was a nudge on his shoulder. It was his best friend, Rufus. Rufus was very shy and pretended to be a toy horse in front of other people. Only Ronnie knew he was real and magical.

"So? Which one do you like the best," asked Rufus?

"Mmm', replied Ronnie, pressing his nose against the window, "that big one there. See?"

He pointed to a window in one of the flats across the street, it WAS a lovely big one.

"What are we waiting for then?" grinned Rufus. Ronnie excitedly clambered on to his friend's back, holding on to the saddle and the reins.

"Wheeee! Here we goooooo," he shouted as Rufus flew out of the window, jumped across the street and landed neatly at the bottom of the pink rainbow. It was real and big and there were so many fluffy clouds everywhere. Rufus started galloping up the rainbow really fast. It was like going up a mountain, except, the road was not grey. It was all the colours he knew and there were sweeties everywhere.

Ronnie reached out to touch the clouds and then licked his fingers. It was candy floss. He grabbed a big bit and when they got to the top of the rainbow, they had a little picnic together. Ronnie could see the rows and rows of buildings from here. He could see the Botanical Gardens, too. They used to go there every Sunday, but now they looked so big and empty. Just like what he had seen on TV.

The two friends played 'I spy' and had lots of fluffy cloud candy, and soon it was time to go home. They decided to slide down the rainbow instead of riding.

"Wheeeee....," shrieked Ronnie.

"Neighghghgh...," whinnied Rufus.

They slid and rolled all the way down, landing with a thud on their bottoms. Back where they had started, on the floor by the window in Ronnie's room.

"That was fun," he shouted, "let's climb the glittery rainbow tomorrow. The one in Suzy's window."

Just then Mum popped her head in to say lunch was ready. She saw her little Ronnie sitting on the floor with his favourite toy horse.

But she did not see the horse wink at Ronnie. And she did not notice his hands were sticky with cloud candy floss!

****

THE PARK

By Jim Morrison

Green swathes of grass criss-crossed by paths,
some straight from beginning to end,
others curve round tree and bush,
leading to hidden surprises.
These paths not empty but populated
by Lowrie-esque figures.
Proud new mothers with new born infants,
gossiping with friends,
exhausted grandparents,
coping with energetic pre-school children,
still learning all that's new in this exciting world.
Into this mix come dog walkers
 and cyclists, trying to weave
a safe path through meandering strollers.
The park where people and animals alike
can breathe fresh air free from
the noise and bustle of urban life.

****

THE LETTER

By Gerry McKendry

Why won't anyone believe me? I have the letter in a secret place at home. While I am here on remand, whatever that means, the final piece of this exciting puzzle could be lying on my doormat. It's not as though I have been recklessly extravagant, a Lambo is not a Ferrari, Bugatti Veyron, or even a Bentley Continental S. Now you can't be seen exiting from a Lamborghini in the clothes I previously wore, so off to Saville Row I went. A few weeks in the Caribbean to show off my new wardrobe is not outrageous, although maybe the private island was a little over the top.

The money I spent was not, of course, stolen, it was borrowed. I think young Carol in the office was surprised, and a little suspicious when I gave her the diamond necklace. I don't know what Ken from the post room meant when he said it only cost him a meal and a couple of drinks.

I planned to take Carol to my new holiday apartment, well if you had the coming in would you not buy a sea-view flat, the sea in question being the Mediterranean, and yes Nice is nice.

To some degree this is all my boss's fault. He was very casual and lackadaisical about giving me access to his American Express card among others. I think this was to say the least ill advised, possibly even foolhardy. My ex-wife said I was incredibly impatient, but when you are about to become a millionaire why wait?

I've always fancied myself as a bit of an Arnold Palmer, I even got a hole in one on the putting green on the front at Skegness. Now I was able, with a little backhander, to jump the waiting list of one of the most prestigious golf clubs in Scotland (no names no pack drill).

I had, of course, no intention to commit embezzlement at any time, after all the funds were only being used temporarily. I was sure that my financial situation would by this stage be such that I could cover all my expenses. So, as you can see, I'm as much a victim in this scenario as anyone else

The police and even my lawyer seem to be inferring that this is a very serious situation. I keep assuring them that not only will I return any money borrowed from the company, but I would be willing to compensate them with a reasonable payment of 'interest' for the short period the funds were at my disposal.

I'm not sure the state supplied lawyer is as good as the QC I first approached, but for some reason he wasn't convinced I could pay *his* bill. I still don't get it. I have it at home, in writing in black and white on a hard copy in the form of a letter, and they still won't take this as collateral for my expenses. Their whole attitude appears to be one of barely hidden amusement and they find my stance as bewildering as I find theirs.

News update: I am at home released on bail and after somewhat feverishly going through the piles of junk mail I was astonished to find no cheque from the 'Readers Digest'. What's keeping it? I was told that I had won a prize up to a million and that my name was on the short list for the top prize.

After a morning of fruitless phone calls to Readers Digest, I began to contemplate my somewhat worrying future when in the afternoon post…salvation. It appears that some Nigerian Prince is prepared to put a fortune in my account if I can send him five thousand for paperwork. My troubles are over. Now I wonder are my boss's Visa or Diner's Club cards still active?

****

THREE WISHES

By Nada Mooney

If a Genie could grant me three wishes
I would never ask for wealth.
Having suffered the dread of the hospital bed
My first wish would be perfect health.

If a Genie could grant me three wishes
A palette and brush I'd employ
To leave behind something of beauty
For all the art-world to enjoy.

If a Genie could grant me three wishes
A wonderful singer I'd be
To gladden the world with my music
Would be my great wish number three

But wishes live only in folklore,
So content, I shall have to be.
I'll simply make do with what I can do
And try to be glad that I'm me.

****

STRAD COLLECTORS

By Walter Sneader

The Lady Blunt Violin made by the luthier Antonio Stradivari (1644-1737) was sold by the Nippon Music Foundation for $15.9 million at an auction in 2011 in order to help victims of the Japanese tsunami. The name of the buyer was not disclosed. Impressive this may be, but most collectors of rare musical instruments believe that there exists an even superior instrument, namely the Messiah Violin, now in the possession of the Ashmolean Museum in Oxford. Its value must be presumed to be well in excess of $30 million, but it has not been put up for sale in recent times.

The two violins just mentioned, together with around 600 others, still exist more than 300 years after they were manufactured. Most of these were made by Antonio Stradivari but some were crafted by his sons Francesco and Ombono. Antonio was born in the vicinity of Cremona, the city where the modern violin was invented by Andrea Amati in the middle of the 16th century. Clearly influenced by Amati and his descendants Antonio made his first violins around 1666. In the 1680s he began to develop instruments that differed from the Amati design. By the middle of that decade the fame of Stradivari was spreading, which encouraged him to experiment with the violins he was making, He increased their length in the 1690s, albeit only by 5/16th of an inch. This, nevertheless, had a dramatic effect on their tone, making it deeper and more fulsome. Other changes he introduced included extending the f - shaped holes in the top plate, flattening of the arch on the back to permit better sound projection in the larger concert halls then being built, and creating sophisticated designs for his scrolls and pegs at the top. By the turn of the 18th century, his golden period is considered to have begun. Violins manufactured by him over the next twenty years are considered by many to be rivalled only by those produced by that other remarkable violin -maker of Cremona, Giuseppe Guarneri (1698-1744).

That so many of the violins produced by Antonio Stradivari have survived to modern times is primarily due to the far-seeking vision of one man, Count Cozio di Salabue (1755-1840). The only son of a distinguished Piedmontese family, he is believed to have developed his interest in the violin from his father who owned and played an Amati. On taking up residence in Turin in 1771 to attend the Military Academy, Cozio became acquainted with the elderly violin-maker Giovanni Guadagnini. Within two years he had made a deal to purchase the output of the craftsman's workshop. Thanks to assistance from Guadagnini, he was subsequently able to buy the entire contents of the Stradivari workshop in Cremona from Antonio's son Paulo in 1775. This featured ten violins created by Antonio Stradivari, including the one later to become known as the Messiah Violin. Also provided in the sale were tools, templates and drawings. This enabled Cozio to develop a greater understanding of the techniques used by Antonio Stradivari. Thanks to publications based on his various notes, scholars have continued to analyse these. Sadly, Cozio and his contemporaries believed they could improve the old violins they possessed. Many that had survived were altered, thereby diminishing their value to collectors.

Following the death of Cozio in 1840, much of his collection was sold to Luigi Tarisio (1796-1854). He was originally a Piedmontese carpenter who enjoyed playing the violin.

Realising that many of them were to be discovered unappreciated all over Northern Italy, he began to collect and take them to Paris where they could be restored, On several of his visits after the acquisition of Count Cozio's collection he talked about a mysterious Stradivarius manufactured in 1716 which had never been played. It acquired the name of the 'Messiah Violin', after the violinist Delphin Alard is reported to have said, "Truly your violin is like the Messiah of the Jews: one always expects him but he never appears."

After the death of Luigi Tarisio, his collection of 144 instruments was purchased in 1855 by Jean Babtiste Vuillaume (1798-1875), the most renowned European violin-maker of the day.

Aware of a rumour that had been circulating amongst dealers in Paris to the effect that Tarisio's collection included a pristine Stradivari from the golden period which had never been played, he travelled in secret to Turin to purchase the entire collection before any of his rivals could lay their hands on it. The collection included 24 of the finest violins made by Antonio Stradivari, of which one was the rare Messiah Violin. Vuillaume then legitimately copied the latter to sell to wealthy clients. Ten years later he sold another one of the Stradivari violins to his student, the polymath Lady Anne Blunt (1837-19170. That this Stradivarius was ultimately to be named after her is surprising since it had been made 116 years before she was born. Like the Messiah Violin it was coloured a characteristic shade of red because most of its original varnish remained intact.

Lady Blunt eventually sold her treasured violin to the German dealer Friedrich Christian Edler very shortly before his death in 1895.

It then came into the hands of the Russian collector of rare instruments, Baron Johann Knoop. He retained it for only five years before releasing it to a wealthy amateur violinist, Mr J E Street of Caterham, who had purchased it for his son, a promising young violinist who was then tragically killed in World War 1. This led to the instrument being sold in1915 to one of the best-known violin collectors of that period, Richard Bennett. He was a Lancashire mill owner who collected rare books, Chinese porcelain and old violins. On his death in 1930 the violin was returned to the renowned London violin dealers W.H.Hills & Sons, who had been involved in some of its earlier sales. That, however, did not put an end to the transfer of the instrument. In 1941, the Swiss collector Henry Werro took possession, retaining it until !959, when an auction at Sotheby's saw it pass to Singaporean millionaire Robin Loft for a bid of $200,000. The following year, 2000, it was purchased by a private collector. Finally, this unknown person allowed the Nippon Music Foundation to take possession of the violin in 2008.

But what became of Vuillaume's Messiah Violin? While owned by Vuillaume, it had been copied many, many times by him and other luthiers. There are said to be millions of violins that have been based on it. Unlike the Lady Blunt violin, the private collectors who took possession of it after Vuillaume's death in 1875 have tended to be publicity-shy. Nevertheless, it provenance since that time has been well established. Suffice to say that it came into the hands of W.H.Hiills & Sons in 1931. Following the outbreak of World War 11 and the London blitz, the company most generously donated it in 1940 tp the Ashmolean Museum in Oxford, with strict stipulations about its preservation, including a warning it must never be played.

While the history of the Messiah Violin since it was obtained by Vuillaume has been properly recorded doubts have repeatedly surfaced over the belief that it was made by Antonio Stradivari in 1716. Scientific investigations were finally introduced to establish its *bona fides,* beginning with dendrochronology, *viz.* the dating of rings in the wood used in its fabrication. In 1998 an eminent German investigator, Peter Kline, claimed that the Messiah violin was a fake because he had dated the wood used in its construction to the year after Antonio Stradivari's death! Two years later, the British endrocrinologists, John Topham and Derek McCormick, using a non-evasive technique in which they compared the wood of many authentic Stradivarius violins with the Messiah, drew the opposite conclusion. The matter was resolved after the Violin Society of America called on a group of independent scientists to investigate. Their findings concluded that Klein was wrong. He then retracted them. Subsequent studies on the varnish as well as computer tomography scans have supported the conclusion that the violin is a genuine Stradivarius from his golden period.

Eminent musicians have long desired to play on violins made by either of the two master craftsmen of Cremona. They are convinced that these are superior to any other violins. Yet for collectors the value of the Messiah and Lady Blunt Violins, two magnificent instruments, lies in their antiquity and original condition rather than their sonority as they have never or rarely been played. Can that be right?

****

FACTION IN CENTRAL BERLIN

By Emily M Clark

The Andersons were sitting in a grassy area in the centre of Berlin. Andy was reading. Emma was enjoying the sun. Wee Billy was looking for something to do.

"What's that big red building, Daddy?" he asked, pointing across the grassland.

"The Municipal buildings," replied Andy. "Now go and practice your maze marching for the Sparks.

Emma looked at Andy's book. *"Waiting for Godot"* she said. "I read that when I was a student. It's about two tramps ..."

"Don't tell me!"

Billy ran back and tugged Andy's tee shirt. "Daddy come and see a bumble bee the size of a bird."

"Show it to your mother."

Emma flicked at a page of Andy's book. "Godot doesn't turn up," she said, "and it's your turn next."

She went to look at Billy's phenomenal bumblebee.

Silence reigned until Billy returned. "Daddy come and see a pink spider the size of a cabbage with two giant claws and a long tail."

"Stop telling fibs."

Daddy it's true, Honest."

*

They joined a small group admiring a giant lobster crawling in the short grass.

"Do you think it escaped from a restaurant?" asked a woman.

"Maybe a dog stole it and dropped it when he got nipped," said a bald man in short shorts.

"It'll die if its not put in water," said Andy.
A German said, "My house is nearby. I will fetch my gardening gloves and pick it up."
"Will you put it into water?" asked Billy
"Yes, I will instruct *die Frau* to put *der hummer* into *wasser* before she cooks my dinner."
Everyone laughed except wee Billy.

****

THE DEMISE OF THE ENCLOPEDIA
By Pamela Duncan

Buried in the deep graveyard of time,
they stand straight-backed
like well-drilled Chelsea Pensioners.
Their red leather jackets uniformly
embossed with gold lettering.
They are the ABC of knowledge
that once spoke volumes.
Discarded now, displaced
by finger-tapping technology,
the cold advancement of a modern age.
Concealed beneath their skin
a wealth of facts rest undisturbed.
They have reached the Autumn of their lives.
Each musty leaf yellows and fades to dust.
As, synonymous with those men of valour
They bravely face the final bullet.

****

BOSNIA

By Kate Richard

Blood toil sweat and tears
But not ours
Bosnian Serb Muslim Croat
A poisonous stew
Of prejudice nationalism hate
But it could not happen here?

Quiet hillsides racked (by tracers
Fire and mortar shells)
We cannot stop them
We send food
You can starve more slowly
We send medicine
You can die less painfully
We may save one little girl
But turn away thousands

You have lost your homes
Your living your hopes
Go away, you have been
Ethnically cleansed.

****

STRANGEST FEELING

By Joyce McKendry

The door opened slowly giving its' usual little creak. Petrified Jane stared at the black space, willing her eyes to become accustomed to the inky darkness, at the same time not wanting to know what was approaching ever so slowly towards the bed where she lay, now bathed in a cold sweat of pure fear. Why hadn't she left the hall light on as usual, she thought desperately as she tried to take control of her soaring feelings of panic. Calm down, breathe slowly, she urged, but by now she was fully aware of a strange dark form gliding silently across the bedroom floor and all efforts to control her horror failed miserably. She opened her mouth to scream, but while she was willing it with all her power, no sound was forthcoming, and the creature was now level with the foot of her bed. She closed her eyes in an effort to summon the last dregs of her strength to scream and, at that precise moment wakened with a great start, sitting upright in her bed, feverishly pulling the corner of her duvet over her mouth.

For a moment or too she was not fully conscious, the feeling of terror still present as she stared fearfully round the room, shadowy in the fast approaching night time gloom. It was a dream, only a dream, she reassured herself as the familiar objects in her bedroom took shape, her eyes adjusting slowly. Switching on her bedside lamp, who knows how long, listening to her heartbeat thundering in her ears until very gradually she accepted that she was safely ensconced in her own bedroom with no bogey man creeping across the floor towards her.

Eventually, she stepped gingerly on to her beloved sheepskin rug reassured by the normality of its soft welcoming feel on her bare feet and slowly made her way to the door, which she now saw in reality was still closed. Carefully she opened it and made her way out into the hall. All was quiet as she had left it before giving in to the strange feeling of fatigue that had beset her earlier, resulting in her unaccustomed nap.

 She switched on the hall light, crossed to the bathroom door, checked all round just to reassure herself, then splashed some water on her face, by which time she was beginning to feel very much better. If only she could shrug off the vague feeling of unreality that still hung over her – it was only a dream, she chided herself, forget it. Slowly she made her way round the flat switching on lights as she went surreptitiously looking in corners, just checking.

Time to start supper she thought, determined to shrug off the unease, Mundane actions – make salad, marinade the chicken, set the table, normality resumed, but still lurking at the back of her mind was the feeling of someone or something lurking just out of sight. After preparing the meal with the chicken to be stir-fried at the last minute, she set the table, poured a glass of wine which she carried into the lounge and settled down to watch TV. Gradually she felt herself relax, managing not to start at every little sound, the light breeze coming in the slightly open window causing the curtain to billow softly. She closed the window and settled once again in front of the TV.

Then she heard the front door open.

"Hi honey, what the hell...." called James, loudly accompanied by the stamping of his foot.

Jane ran to the door to be greeted by James looking furiously down the path.

"That bloody cat from No. 5 again, frightened the daylight out of me rushing out like that. Has he been in here all day again?" he asked.

"I don't know how he manages to get in," said Jane giving a little smile, and thought to herself well so much for a strange lurking presence. "I'll just finish supper. You sit down then I'll bring you a glass of wine."

She strode into the kitchen ready to put the stir-fry into the wok to be greeted by an empty bowl with a hole carefully punched through the stretched clingfilm cover.

Not only was the visiting cat gone, but so was the chicken carefully prepared for the evening meal, adding insult to injury.

That darned cat frightened the life out of two sensible adults, albeit in different ways, but he was now on his merry way without a backward glance, well fed on a pound of best chicken breast.

****

A TRIP DOWN MEMORY LANE

By Myrna Sneader

Looking back for a trip down memory lane my recollection of happy times camping and caravanning immediately come to mind. There were many wonderful holidays in our own country as well as in France between 1963 and 1982.

My first glimpse of any camp was a Scout one in Blackwaterfoot , Arran. That was when my husband, the scoutmaster, first showed me he could cook. This effort was to be his last. He made a dish called 'grew'. On the final day, just before the scouts left and I arrived, all the remaining unused food was combined in a large Billy-can. It then just grew and grew, hence the name.

My own introduction to tent camping was in a bivouac, a small two-person skimpy tent purchased from Black's in Union Street, Glasgow. Despite its fragility, it withstood a fierce storm during that first weekend. We had pitched it somewhere off the A9 near Pitlochry. I managed to enjoy the experience despite the awful weather. Not long after we upgraded it to a proper framed tent, doubtless encouraged by my prompting.

Our summer holidays usually began when school broke up. This was considerably cheaper as English schools were not yet closed. June was always hectic for me as a teacher with all sorts of things to be done before the end of term.

Though I was exhausted, we sometimes headed off literally straight from school. I would take with me beautiful flowers received from my little pupils, even if the lilies might stain the car upholstery.

Nearby campers must have thought it a bit eccentric to decorate our tent with flowers.

As you might expect, our Ford Mondeo was filled to the brim. The baby bath was even strapped to the roof. To drive safely we had to depend on the side mirrors as nothing could be seen through baggage blocking any view out of the back window.

We cooked our meals on a gas-fuelled stove. How I always looked forward to being served in a decent restaurant on the way home. Never will I forget the occasion when we had intended to have dinner in Lockerbie.

Arriving late, we found our choice of restaurants limited to a very run-down chippie on Main Street. Surprising the staff by asking where we could wash our hands before eating, we were directed to a bathroom. To our astonishment we were told the sink could not be used as it was cracked. The waitress apologised as she lifted a huge tray of fish from the bath. Now we could wash.

We returned to the main room to be served. There were chips with everything. I don't exaggerate. The plates were chipped, the cups, too. And a few extra ones came with the fish.

I don't think I will ever forgive my husband for that visit. He had promised earlier that we would find somewhere nice on the way home from the Lake District. Well, at least it was unforgettable. But, for me, the term 'Lockerbie disaster' still has two meanings.

In 1974, we graduated to a caravan. This was true luxury in comparison to the tent. It even had running water and a tiny toilet.

Our closest friends also became keen caravaners. We never travelled in convoy as that would have irritated motorists. And, of course, we joined the Caravan Club. That way we knew which sites were the best to stay at.

Once when we visited the Dordogne, we were informed on arrival that our friends had phoned to say they would be delayed by a couple of days. We missed their eventual arrival until there was a knock on our door. When they said they were pitched next door to us, we looked out but could not see their van. There was only a shiny new one there. Imagine our amazement when our friends walked into it! Their explanation was bizarre. They told us that their caravan had been written off after flipping over when they were overtaking a car at 60mph on an autoroute. A phone call to tell their insurance company had resulted in them being able to buy a replacement in France. They had explained that this avoided running up a huge hotel bill for the insurance company to pay.

Homeward bound, our vans had to join a queue of caravans at the docks in Calais waiting to pass through customs prior to boarding the channel ferry. Reaching the front of it we watched what was happening to the driver ahead. He was arguing with a customs officer. They both entered his van and a moment or two later he came out holding four bottles of liquor. He angrily smashed them to the ground, shouting that if he couldn't have them nobody else would.

Next it was our friends' turn. When the customs officer turned round. he asked if there was anything to declare. The reply was a flick of the thumb pointing backwards. The official looked puzzled until he heard the glib response, "The caravan."

The expression on that custom officer's face was quite something.
He muttered, "Mon dieu!" and gasped.
There was a long delay.
We had many wonderful holidays in our little Sprite caravan. In the evenings we would join our friends in their more luxurious van while our kids played board games.in ours. These were great times. We explored much of France, the only downside being that our kids did not see the inside of a 'plane until they outgrew the caravan. It is ironical that one of them was later to be awarded a certificate by British Airways to say that he was the most frequent flier of the year.
Will the post-Coronavirus world see caravan holidays becoming de rigour for all families? Only time will tell.

****

THE MAGICIAN

By Gerry McKendry

There was a magician called Gerry.
whose jacket was red as a cherry.
When he heard someone snoring
He asked, "Am I boring?"
And the whole ruddy crowd shouted, "VERY!"

****

FREDA AND THE FAIRY QUEEN

By Emily M Clark

Freda and her parents lived in a log cabin in the woods. Her father was a woodcutter and her mother was a school teacher.

"Last night I dreamed about the Fairy Queen," said Freda at supper.

"Was she beautiful?" asked her mother.

"Very beautiful. She wore a pink dress and silver slippers. I could see through her wings."

"A fairy's wings are made of gossamer," said her mother.

"The Fairy Queen said I could make a wish."

"I could do with a new chainsaw," said her father.

"I woke up before I could make a wish."

"Your father's joking about a chainsaw, Freda. If you dream about the Fairy Queen again have your wish ready."

For once, Freda did not complain when her mother said it was time for bed. Soon, she was dreaming about being in the woods surrounded by bluebells. With a fluttering sound the Fairy Queen appeared. This time her dress was lilac and her slippers were purple. She scattered fairy dust, turning the bluebells pink.

"Have you thought about your wish, Freda?" asked the Fairy Queen.

"I have Your Majesty."

"What is your wish?"

"I wish for my family to spend Christmas day in the Palace of Russia with the Tsar and Tsarina."

The Fairy Queen began to raise her wand and stopped. "Your wish requires a lot of magic, Freda. I will ask the Fairy King to help."

*

"The woodcutter's daughter has made a wish," the Fairy Queen told her husband.

"I hope she's not one of the greedy ones," said the Fairy King, "How old is she?"

"I often watch Freda playing in the woods. She's six or seven and I'm sure she's not greedy."

"Humans have no time for us," said the Fairy King. "They're too busy with computer games and electronics, Anyway, what did the child wish for?"

"Freda wants her family to spend Christmas at the Palace of Russia."

"Why can't she wish for something simple, like a doll or Nintendo?"

"Will you help me to make her wish come true?"

"I suppose so. We'll put on our thinking caps and see what we can do."

*

Freda and her parents were decorating the Christmas tree. They looked at each other when a car stopped outside the cabin.

Freda ran to the window. "It's a silver car," she said.

Her father opened the door to a tall stranger. "Please come in," he said. "We seldom have visitors here."

"Thank you," said the man and stepped inside.

"Are you lost?" asked Freda's mother.

"No, not lost. I have an invitation for you from the Tsar and Tsarina."

"There must be some mistake," said Freda's father.

"There is no mistake. You are invited to spend Christmas at the Palace of Russia."

"But we have no suitable clothes to wear," said Freda's mother.

"A dressmaker will take care of that. On Christmas Eve be ready at seven. I will drive you to the palace for an overnight stay."

"A sleepover at the palace," said Freda and jumped up and down.

For the first time the stranger smiled. "Yes, you may call it that."

*

On Christmas morning at the palace a dressmaker brought a selection of beautiful clothes. Freda's mother chose a blue velvet gown with a silver belt. Silver shoes with small heels were a perfect fit. And Freda's father looked very handsome in black trousers and a white shirt. His woodcutter's boots were exchanged for black leather shoes. Freda's choice was a lilac dress and pink slippers, like the Fairy Queen had worn in the dream.

The dressmaker was pleased because the clothes fitted so well. She instructed the family on how to behave when presented to the royal couple.

"You must bow or curtsy. Do not speak unless you are asked a question."

*

Freda stared at the food on the long table in the banqueting hall. There were countless turkeys, hams and roasts. Every kind of fruit was piled high in crystal bowls. Servants, dressed in black and white, served steaming soup from silver tureens.

As guests of honour the family were seated next to the Tsar and Tsarina. The dressmaker had advised to watch others if they were unsure which cutlery to use.

"Do you know why you are here?" the Tsar asked Freda, as he dipped a silver spoon into his soup.

Freda was unsure if she should mention the Fairy Queen and the wish.

"Well I'll tell you," continued the Tsar. "My wife had a strange dream. In the dream, she was told to invite a woodcutter's family for Christmas."

Now, the Tsarina spoke to Freda. "In my dream, I was told to grant you a wish. But, to ask for this wish, you may use only one word."

Freda looked at the beautiful Tsarina. How impossible it seemed to ask for a wish in a single word.

"One word," repeated the Tsarina, "and I will grant your wish."

Down the endlessly long table, people stopped eating their soup. They stared at Freda and waited and waited and waited. Freda thought and thought and thought. "Share," she said at last, looking along the food laden table.

"Well done," said the Tsarina. "We will share."

"Yes," said the Tsar, "We will share everything with our people in Russia."

The Tsar and Tsarina are now beloved throughout Russia. And all because of Freda's two wishes."

****

THE BEGINNING

By Pamela Duncan

Alice came to me on a dreary November morning like a light from above.

"Dr Holdsworth, I was told at the university you were looking for someone to help with the dogs," she said. "I'm a PHD veterinary student supporting myself through the course. What with digs and books, I've just got to find a job."

This girl was pleading. She needed work as much as I needed help. She was small, slight with short dark hair, not the least bit like Paula to whom I'd been married for eighteen years. Happily, I thought, until she left saying simply, "I'm going, Frank."

"Going? Where to?"

She'd blurted it out. I'd been so selfishly wrapped up in my work I hadn't noticed. Paula and Mark, the man I considered my best friend. The betrayal was twofold. Inwardly, I'd fallen apart those first few weeks but I'd numbed my feelings sufficiently to convince the university I could still operate as Head of the Chemistry Department. But for my son, Robin, and the need to devote extra time to a new project, I might have gone under.

The dogs Alice referred to were the twenty-four spaniels I kennelled and bred – a lifetime hobby. In recent years, Paula had shouldered the hard grind while I dealt with the servicing and showing and lapped up the glory. At the age of twelve, Robin chose to stay with me when his mother left and he lent a hand, but it wasn't enough.

The girl was waiting for my response.

"What's your name?" I asked.

"Alice James."

"Age?"

"Twenty-five."

That surprised me as I had placed her some four years younger.

"Well, Alice," I said, "we do need someone badly. Robin, my son, does his best but it's not good for him to be tied down. I'll show you around first, then we might come to some arrangement."

My home bordered isolated farm lands and had at one time been the farmhouse. It sprawled through eight single storey apartments and was sited amid a couple of acres of garden and field.

The kennels spread across a third of the land and I watched Alice traipse round them. Though the paths were puddled and muddy, she didn't hesitate as rain beaded her small, dark head. The dogs yapped and barked their usual chorus. Strangers were rarely friends until they'd proved themselves, but Alice worked magic as she calmed them with her voice and hands.

"They like you," I said. "That's a good omen."

"Animals are my life," she replied simply.

We went into the house to talk. The dogs weren't the only things in need of attention. I was acutely aware of the clutter in my kitchen, but Alice appeared not to notice.

"Coffee?" I asked and she accepted it sweet and black, the way I liked it myself.

Robin came up the drive on his bicycle and waved through the kitchen window. A tall well-built lad, he registered surprise at seeing Alice. I explained about her offer to help with the dogs.

"Great," he said, and meant it.

"When can you start?" I asked Alice.

"Tomorrow. I've a couple of lectures in the morning then I'm free."

We agreed to four three-hourly sessions during the week and all day Sundays at a modest pay of £10 an hour plus meals and expenses for the use of her moped.

Soon, I became accustomed to her figure mucking out the kennels, exercising the dogs. All the jobs Puala had grown to hate. Her ability to handle the animals gave me confidence and Robin, too, seemed to enjoy her company. All our lives jogged along without many complications and I concentrated on my project to such an extent the hurt caused by Paula and Mark faded.

Within the year my divorce was finalised, granted to Paula unopposed on the grounds of mental stress. So that was how she summed up our years together. A few months later, with a baby already conceived, she married Mark and a full bloodied stop wiped my slate clean.

Alice passed her final exams. It had taken eighteen months of hard work to gain her doctorate.

"Please come to my graduation?" she asked and I agreed, feeling a distinct sense of pride, as if I'd been part of her achievement.

After the ceremony, we dined at The Park Gallery, a delightfully expensive restaurant renowned for good food, wine and soft lights. Apart from the odd dog show, it was the first time we'd been out together. I listened to her soft voice as we discussed everything from the kennels to the universe. We laughed in a way I hadn't done for years. A sense of intimacy kindled and sparkled within me.

To think I'd hardly noticed how beautiful she was. The curve of her chin, the slight tilt of her nose, her lips moist and full and those dark brown eyes reflecting the candlelight. At twenty-seven, as she now was, Alice was just young enough to be my daughter, but the feelings she aroused in me that night were far from fatherly. They scared me. I'd have to fight them, for I was sure there was no way they'd be reciprocated. Alice would find someone her own age.

The following day, Alice approached me. "I've a business proposition to discuss with you, Frank. I'm considering setting up a veterinary practice and I'll need premises. Could I take over two rooms at the rear of your house as a bed-sit and surgery? That way I could still attend to the kennels."

The scheme was so simple and practical I applauded it. "Of course. Robin will have to clear out his rubbish, but it sounds a great idea."

I struggled to hide my feelings of elation. To have Alice staying under my own roof, to see her every single day was beyond belief. Since her graduation, I sensed a relaxation in our friendship but didn't dare to read more into it. I knew I loved her, yet it was impossible to conceive that a girl her age could regard a middle-aged professor as anything other than a boring old trout. I resolved to continue to keep my emotions under control and when she came to stay the rein would be tightened.

Alice and I worked together to adapt the new veterinary surgery and Robin was never far away.

"Guess we'll have all sorts of creatures coming here for treatment," he said. "Might even get a crocodile."

"That," Alice smiled, "is highly unlikely."

"But you never know," my son said, hopefully

I bought Alice a distinctive brass plate to attach to the rear entrance that was now hers. Time flew as her reputation with animals increased. If anything, I saw less of Alice than before, but I felt comforted knowing she was nearby. Occasionally, we ate together and talked late into the night. I ached for her not to return to her own rooms but she always did, though sometimes I felt she was reluctant to leave.

Robin was approaching fifteen and frequently stayed overnight with friends in the village. From time to time he joined his mother and Mark and his young half-brother in Seddington. Alone in the house, Alice and I remained firmly in our own quarters.

Another six months passed. The dogs continued to thrive and having a vet on call for the odd emergency proved very convenient. My dogs showed well and gathered trophies throughout the country. It had never occurred to me to breed other animals until Alice asked if she could keep a horse in the far field.

"Misty's a lovely mare. She belongs to one of my clients who is retiring. There's a snag. She's not cheap and she's in foal. Due around the end of March. I've looked after her for some time and I reckon I can scrape together the asking price."

I considered before answering positively. "Why not have a horse? There's room for stabling. I've always fancied owning the winner of the Gold Cup."

"Start at the top, eh? Thanks. You've no idea what this means to me." She leant forward and I thought she was going to kiss me, but instead she gave me a brief hug. I could smell the freshness of her skin and felt the softness of her hair as it brushed my cheek.

"I'll see if I can round up a stallion for us, as well," I said.

Oh, Alice, if only you - I didn't finish the unspoken thought. I was still afraid the wrong move would end my blissful, if incomplete, existence for ever.

The cost of the horses was significant but not prohibitive. Robin was in his element.

"They are magnificent," he said, as he rode Drachma and led Misty over the field each evening.

February came and with it an invitation to the Grand University Staff Dinner, a formal occasion that gathered Professors, their wives and partners from all over the country. I asked Alice to join me and she seemed delighted and I booked a taxi.

Alice came to my lounge, her midnight blue dress shimmered as it flirted with her wasp-like waist.

"You look very lovely tonight," I said and restrained myself from taking her in my arms.

"And you look extremely handsome. Evening wear suits you." And, this time, she did kiss me very lightly on the cheek. I felt my heart race and my face flush. "Now I've embarrassed you," she smiled.

I wanted to tell her to embarrass me again and again but my tongue was tied like an infantile schoolboy's.

At that moment, Robin burst into the room. "It's Misty. I think she's having the foal. You'll have to come."

"But she's not due for another couple of weeks."

Alice dashed to the surgery and returned with her bag and we raced after my son through the darkness to the stables and knelt beside the mare in all our finery.

Robin ran back to the house for extra covers as Alice delved into her bag and pulled out her long surgical gloves. "I can't believe it. She showed no signs earlier today. Her first and she's making it this easy."

Robin reappeared with blankets. "Dad, there's a taxi driver wants to know when you're coming."

"Give him the money on the sideboard. Tell him we're sorry. It should be enough to send him away happy." Robin glanced across at Misty "Do I need to come back?" "No, son, you look after the house." Robin left gratefully. The stable was lit by one old coach lantern which cast long shadows against the narrow walls. In the semi-light, Alice appeared haloed. An angel, I thought, my angel. Her words came softer than ever. "You're doing fine, Misty girl. Keep it up. Not long now." Her calmness encouraged Misty. I, myself, was churning inside. Beads of perspiration broke on my forehead, matching the sweat that glistened on the coat of the mare. Gently, Alice helped Misty ease her foal into the world. I knelt in wonder at her side. The foal lay for a few minutes before slowly raising itself to stand wobbly-legged. "Here, son, suckle," Alice coaxed and foal and mother bonded.

An awe of silence hung in the stable that only the heavy breathing of the mare and the suckling of her foal broke until Alice leapt to her feet, stripped off the bloodstained gloves and ran her hands under the water tap.

"A son. Misty has a son. Our very first foal," she cried. Her shimmering dress was covered with wisps of straw and the knees of my suit were mud stained. Elated by our efforts, we fell into each other's arms. The pent-up emotion of years released as I held and caressed her. Suddenly, it dawned on me what I was doing and I broke away.

"Alice, dear, darling Alice, I'm so sorry." She stroked my hair. "There's no need to be, Frank. I've loved you from the start. We've wasted so long."

Robin came back into the stables. "I couldn't relax down at the house," he explained. He patted the tiny foal. "It's all over," he sighed.

"No, Robin," I replied. "It's just beginning."

****

SAFFRON

By Nada Mooney

I opened the door and she walked in, head held high, tail ramrod straight: a queen among cats – a total stranger. It would have been an insult to call her ginger for she was golden and stately in her bearing. We called her Saffron. She wore no collar and it was before household pets were chipped. We took photographs and put them in local shops and in the free newspaper. But all to no avail. She remained a mystery.

Our own much-loved Lucy, whose brood of five gorgeous kittens had been successfully homed, had met her end under a coal lorry so the children were desperate to keep Saffron. I felt she must have come from a caring environment because she was in such perfect condition. I begged the children not to think she was ours until every effort had been made to find her true owner.

Weeks passed and nobody claimed her so we asked the vet to check her over. He declared her to be in perfect health. She had probably had kittens but she had been spayed. We were no nearer to discovering her origins so she stayed with us.

In keeping with her bearing she was a fussy and fastidious eater. We soon learned what she did and did not like.

Cheap tinned fish got an angry swish of her tail and look of disgust. She was passionate about prawns which occasionally came her way if we ourselves happened to be indulging in that particular seafood treat.

A territorial cat, in every way, she kept a strict watch on the garden. Woe betide any marauding tom or curious kitty who dared to invade her space. They were speedily charged with hissing and spitting and the occasional bat round the ears.

Instead of 'What's for eating?' the children would cone in from school and say 'Where's Saffy?' Often they buried their faces in her soft fur and whispered secrets, while she sat sphinx-like narrowing her amber eyes and purring softly – never moving before they did.

She didn't like to be picked up and would decide whether or not she wished to be stroked. We actually felt honoured if she jumped up onto our lap. In many ways the household revolved around her. Such was her remarkable personality. Always attuned to the mood of the family she could dissipate presence and scolding little yelps and all would be resolved in a short time.

A cat-flap was installed, but Saffron preferred to come and go by the kitchen window, where she tapped until someone let her in or out. There were mishaps galore – curiosity resulted in a fall from an upstairs window, being shut in the washing machine and narrowly missing a fatal fall when she chased a squirrel up a very tall tree.

Saffron lived to be eighteen and died in her sleep one night, thereby sparing us the dreadful decision of making that final visit to the vet. Lying peacefully with a favourite toy between her front paws we had to accept our loss. We knew instinctively she could never be replaced.

She has a special place in the garden where we planted a golden rosebush which becomes more beautiful with every passing year.

****

NO COLD CALLERS

Nada Mooney

I think most people's biggest moan
When they lift the telephone
Is to be told that they have won
A nice vacation in the sun

But the small print gets no mention
Than is never their intention
Their prize is to catch the unwary
With time-share deals so very scary

Then there's the poshly spoken lass
Who tries to sell you lots of glass
And isn't even slightly fazed
When you say your telly's double-glazed

But on your door step it is worse
And I will mouth a silent curse
The man who just came in your gate
Will promise an amazing rate

For work he says he can complete
In record time within the week
It's only then you smell a rat
And know exactly what he's at.

He wants a trip to the local bank
Your lucky stars you have to thank
For common sense you do not lack
Your head don't button up the back!

So he can be sent upon his way
No better off as you won't pay
But call the police to pull their ranks
And stop this conman and his pranks

Religious zealots I really detest
They are such a serious pest
My daughter says avoid their tricks
The real Watchtower's by Jimi Hendrix

So cold callers I do not want
But my wishes I can flaunt
That family and friends do stop here
Because to me they are so dear.

****

THE ROSE

By Pamela Duncan

Plucked from its unyielding stem,
I cupped the delicate blossom to my face,
and saw within the tears of morning dew,
and sensed the fragrance of a rose in bloom.

****

BEWARE OF KELPIES

By Ann Morrison

Throwing another log on the fire, Andrew stood watching the sparks shower up the chimney. His wife, Isabel, pulled the heavy curtains, shutting out the storm that was raging across the island.

"Come in nearer the fire," Andrew said to his father. "Here let me top up your glass."

Duncan McPherson gladly accepted the whisky and settled down on the settee between his two grandchildren.

"Dad, there's no way you're going to drive home tonight. I'm away to make up the bed in the spare room," Isobel told the old man, before turning to her children. "Will you two kindly put away those blinkin' phones?"

"Okay," Thomas, the eldest and cheekiest said with a grin. "The reception's rubbish, anyway." Then, addressing his grandfather in the Gaelic. "Great that you're staying, Shener. Will you tell us one of your stories?"

"And what would you be wanting a story about on a night like this?" his grandfather wondered, as he savoured his dram beside the warm fire.

"Miss was telling us about Kelpies in school today," young Morag replied.

"Was she now. And I hope she told you to give them a wide berth if ever you should come across them. You must beware of Kelpies."

"She said one day we may cross the mainland and see them. They're in Falkirk."

"Yes, that's right. I've seen pictures of the ones they have there and magnificent sculptures they are, too. But don't we have the real ones right here on the island? Don't Kelpies live in every loch in Scotland? Beautiful beasts, no doubt about that, but dangerous, as a lovely maiden found out on just such a night as this."

Once Isobel was seated and Andrew had handed her a glass, his father began.

"Many years ago, there lived in these parts a King who had a beautiful daughter. Her skin was white as milk and her hair, that hung half-way down her slender body, glowed like a summer sunset. She wasn't just lovely this Princess, she was also good and kind.

One Autumn day when the sky was a clear blue and the leaves on the trees looked like God had emptied his paint over them, she was walking through the woods when she came across an old woman busily gathering brambles. The woman was bent over the bushes trying to reach the biggest, juiciest fruit. The ones that I'm sure you'll agree always seem to be at the very back.

"Can I help you?" the Princess asked.

"Thank you," the old woman replied, but I don't want you to get your dress torn by the thorns."

"I'll be careful," the Princess laughed, taking the basket from the woman's hands and stretching to pick the best of the fruit.

Soon she was able to hand the filled basket back to the old woman, who tutted in horror at the bramble juice stains on the girl's white hands.

"You'll need lemon juice to get those stains off," she fussed. "Although where you would get that here I don't know."

The Princess smiled. It seemed the old woman hadn't recognised her. One such tree, a gift from a Spanish sailor, who had been rescued when his ship floundered on the rocks, grew in the shelter of the castle garden.

"Don't worry, I'll be fine," the Princess assured her. "Anyway, I enjoyed meeting you. Are you going to make lots of jam?"

"Not jam. I've a secret recipe for special syrup that cures folks suffering with coughs and colds when winter blows in. If ever you should find you need some, come by my cottage at the edge of the sea loch. I'll have a bottle of it waiting for you."

With that the old lady thanked the Princess for her help and was on her way.

Now, sometime later, when the nights had drawn in and the wild Atlantic gales were buffeting the island, the Queen took ill with a terrible cold. The poor lady's throat was so sore she could hardly swallow the possets the castle cook made for her. They tried everything they could think of to make her more comfortable, but nothing seemed to work.

One evening the King suggested juice from the lemons that were carefully stored in the kitchen larder might help. That was when the Princess remembered the old woman. Perhaps some syrup would be soothing for her mother's throat. She would get some to surprise her.

Telling no one, she wrapped herself in her warmest cloak and slipped out into the dark night. Mindful of the uneven ground, she relied on the roar of the sea and taste of salt in the air to guide her towards the loch and the old woman's cottage.

She was almost there when the moon suddenly appeared from behind the scudding clouds, lighting up the path before her. That was when she saw it, standing there under the cliffs as still as the sculptures they have in Falkirk, a beautiful white horse.'

"Was it a Kelpie, Shener?" Morag asked, her eyes shining in the firelight.

"It was my pet. Now if you listen a bit more, I'll tell you why to keep away if you happen to come across one." The little girl snuggled further into her grandfather as he continued. 'The horse gleamed like silver in the moonlight. Its mane and tail shone like spun silk. It was by far the most magnificent animal the Princess had ever seen. Desperate to get a closer look she quietly moved nearer. The horse neighed and made off towards an opening in the rocks.'

"I didn't know there was a cave there," the Princess thought as she followed it along the beach.

What she found was no ordinary cave, but a magical grotto, the walls of which were covered in intricate patterns made from sea shells. There were mussels and cockles, crabs and clams, oysters and buckies. In the centre of the cave was a deep pool, its ripples reflected round the walls.

Standing at the edge of the pool was the beautiful horse. It seemed to be inviting the Princess to come nearer as it stretched out its long neck while whinnying gently. Fascinated, the girl moved towards the horse. Holding out her hand, eager to stroke its soft nose.

Now what she didn't know was that Kelpies are covered in an invisible cloak of the stickiest substance known to man. If someone should touch one of them there is no way they can get free. The kelpie has them in its power.

The wicked beasts run into the sea and drown their victim, then they eat them. "

Just as the Princess was about to stroke what she believed was a wonderful horse, a voice rang out.

"Don't touch."

Startled the Princess turned to see the old lady who had been picking brambles running into the grotto brandishing a large cast iron cooking pot. Lifting her arm, the woman threw the pot at the horse. There was a flash as of lightening and, with a mighty roar, the horse jumped into the pool and disappeared.

"Why did you do that?" the Princess asked, weeping for the animal she feared had drowned.

"Don't go wasting your tears on a Kelpie, lass," the old lady told her. "They might look beautiful, but they are evil beasts that have lured many a young man and woman to their death. If you had touched it, I would have needed to cut your finger off to set you free. It would have taken you with it into the pool and out under sea where it would have had you for its supper. Yes, many have ended up that way. The only thing that scares them off is iron, and luckily I had my old cooking pot to hand when I heard it whinnying."

The terrified Princess followed the old woman to her cottage. Once the girl calmed down, she explained how the Queen was ill and how, remembering about the bramble syrup, she wondered if some of it might help.

"I'd be honoured if you'd take some of my soup for your mother," the old woman answered.

"You do know who I am?" the Princess stammered.

"I know lots of things, my dear. Now let's get you home.

The still shaking Princess did not remember much about getting home, just that the old woman took her hand and guided her safely through the dark tangle of woods.

At breakfast, the Queen managed to swallow some of the syrup.

"That was like magic, Darling," She told her daughter. "Honestly, I feel better already."

"I'm so glad," smiled the Princess, thinking to herself that was probably just what it was.

"Goodness, Shener, was the old lady a fairy?"

"Who knows? The Princess searched for the cottage to thank her properly, and for the grotto. But she never found either of them again. Still, doesn't it just go to show how one good turn deserves another? The Princess helped the old woman and she in turn helped the Princess's mother. I've told you a story. That's my good turn. Do you think maybe your dad will return the compliment and give me another dram?"

****

BEHIND CLOSED DOORS

By Anjana Sen

When we sat shielding behind closed doors
We didn't just stand staring at our dirty floors.
We wrote and read and shared on Zoom.
We met and spoke to shake off gloom,
And the Anthology was born through this driving force.

When she sat shielding behind closed doors
She wasn't just staring at cluttered floors.
An idea grew from a tiny bud.
Stories and poems landed with a thud
And this Anthology was born through her driving force

****

THE GRANDFATHER

By Emily M Clark

"He's dead," John told the constable who was waiting outside the private ward.

"Did Mr Milosevik say anything?"

"It was…personal," replied John, still surprised at being asked for forgiveness.

"The detectives will have to question you about the body buried in the woods."

The grandfather's elderly neighbour opened the door as John walked up the path. "How is he?" she asked.

"He's dead."

Her face turned white. "Oh … I don't know what to say, John."

"You don't have to say anything, Miss Cameron. We both know what he was like."

He unlocked the storm doors of the villa. Moth eaten umbrellas and muddy boots cluttered the vestibule. The smell of cheroots met him.

He climbed the stairs to his old attic bedroom and switched on the light, fingers easily finding the switch as they did long ago. A bare light- bulb on a corded flex spread a dim light.

The walls were a khaki colour as if the painter had no imagination or was restricted by the mean old man.

He peered through dirty windows with aspects of a tree-lined garden. The rope swing of his childhood, rotted and frayed, undulated from an oak branch.

The nicotine-stained villa sparked memories of his grandfather's breath. And painful memories of damaged ligaments caused by an arm twisted up his back and a broken leg from being hauled off the swing.

His grandfather got angry when he asked about his mother or his grandmother.

"How many times do I have to tell you? Your grandmother ran away with another man and took Lisa with her."

"Who was my father? And where are they now?"

*

The funeral was a bleak affair with no mourners apart from John and Miss Cameron.

"Come to my house for something to eat, John, she invited as they left the graveside.

"Only if it's something quick. I've an assessor coming to look at a painting."

"Five minutes to heat some chicken broth. Sit in the lounge and I'll bring it through."

The ancient lounge evoked more memories. The settee with floral covers, still here, thin and faded now. He had often slept on it after a beating from his grandfather. When he went back next door it was as if nothing had happened.

"Get your homework done," the old man would bark in his Serbian accent. "or your teachers will complain."

Miss Cameron's voice brought him back to the present.

"Will you manage the soup on a tray, John, or would you rather eat in the kitchen?"

"I'm used to eating off a tray and watching TV," laughed John.

When the soup was finished, Miss Cameron took the dishes into the kitchen. She returned with a bottle of whisky and a bottle of sherry. "I think we need a drink, John."

He was about to refuse when he saw tears behind the horn- rimmed glasses. "Make it a whisky, with water."

"John that body in the woods is your grandmother," she said, handing him a generous whisky.

"But it can't be her. She left with another man and took my mother with her."

"That's what he told everyone."

John took a sip of whisky and waited for her to continue.

"You were a month old when your mother rang my bell, her face bruised and bleeding. He'd killed your grandmother and Lisa had to get away before he killed her, too. She begged me to take you to safety. Ten minutes after she'd gone, the door smashed open and he took you away. I was too scared to phone the police. After midnight, I saw flickering among the trees. I knew he was burying your grandmother."

"Do you think my grandfather is…?"

"I know what you're thinking and the answer's no. Lisa was attacked when she was sixteen, resulting in pregnancy. She'll be forty-six now."

*

"It's not a genuine Rossetti," said the professor who had arrived promptly. "It's an excellent copy and I'll give you a fair price for it."

"Grandfather maintained it was genuine."

"It's very rare to find a genuine PRB painting. They're always being copied."

"PRB, I don't …?"

"Pre-Raphaelite Brotherhood, founded by Rossetti."

"After the disappointment, John prised open his grandfather's desk. Among the receipts and papers was a bundle of envelopes addressed to John Milosevic. Most of them were birthday cards but the last envelope contained a letter with an address in Via Reggio, Italy.
'You are sixteen, John, and almost a man. I enclose my address and phone number in the hope that one day you will contact me. It's just too painful to write any more cards. This comes with much love from your mother, Lisa Milos.
John picked up the old Bakelite phone and dialled the number on the card.
"Buon giorno," said a young female voice.
"Good afternoon. My name is John Milosevic. Can I speak to Lisa Milosevic, please?"
"Santo cielo! Mamma mia!
Johm listened to the excited voices in the background."
Madre! Madre! Pronto! Il miracola!"
"Che's su al telefono?"
"Il figlio Mia fratello, John."
The phone was picked up. " Is it really you, John?"
John smiled before he answered, picturing himself driving for Milan to Via Reggio on a Vespa scooter. Absolutely nothing could stop him from making this journey to meet his new family.

****

MEANDERINGS

By Pamela Duncan

I am sitting at my desk staring at a large, blank sheet of paper. To my right lies a pile of Biro pens. Randomly, I select one. It happens to be dark blue, reminiscent of my mood, I think.

At this moment my mind is as blank as the paper, but I start to draw a line. From the foot of the sheet, it threads its way towards the top. At first, it runs straight, then begins to meander, winding left, then right, repeating the pattern until it reaches the top edge.

A second's pause and the Biro takes off again. It is in charge, My hand has no control as it retraces its steps down the sheet.

Its path becomes erratic, sweeping across the white surface as if crazed, backwards and forwards, creating a frenzy of lines. Halfway down the sheet, those lines become circles. Swirling as they form a spaghetti junction. The movement is frantic. The result dramatic.

The Biro calms down and slowly continues its passage towards the bottom edge of the paper.

Before reaching it, it swerves violently left and its movement quickens as it zig-zags upwards, pausing briefly to divert right to form a triangular shape with three solid sides. There is no obvious exit. Frustrated, the Biro forces its way through and, emerging triumphantly, makes a dash to the top of the sheet.

The thick blue line comes to a halt and pulls up beside the spaghetti circles. It is a breath away from entering the mass of rings. Fear of becoming entangled causes it to draw back.

It veers further right, before heading to the top, where it turns around and proceeds in an orderly diagonal line across the surface from top to bottom. It takes flight to the opposite corner and sketches a second diagonal line, this time from bottom to top to form a cross.

Only then does the Biro hesitate. The cross has condemned and deleted all the meanderings, the circles, the triangle and the erratic lines. It no longer is in control. My hand can dictate the next move, clearly and concisely.

I stare down at the pattern in front of me. It would appear to have no meaning until it dawns on me. These meanderings speak volumes. They express the workings of an over-active brain. They capture the fluctuations, the twists and turns of a full and varied life. They reflect who I was and who I am.

My hand is in control as it replaces the Biro back among the pile and turns the sheet over. The surface facing me is blank, ready to be filled. I pick another Biro from the pile. This one is red. The colour of fire and inspiration.

****

THE BEST LAID SCHEMES

By Nada Mooney

Adam was in love. Totally besotted. He couldn't sleep, couldn't eat – well, not as much as usual and he would waken at night in a cold sweat lest some wittier, richer or better looking fellow might steal his darling away.

A bank loan had secured a dainty antique ring of rubies and diamonds set in rose gold – suitable he felt for a girl like Rachel

Her birthday was next week and he hadn't dropped as much as a hint of his intentions, only promising a lovely meal in La Casa Dolce, where his friend Kenny worked.

Kenny, flamboyant and, outgoing, in complete contrast to Adam, was studying law and supplementing his grant with his part-time job.

Sipping beer in their local the boys were catching up with each other's news, when Adam outlined his plan.

"I've made the booking and the rest is up to you, so *please* Kenny, don't let me down."

Kenny looked serious and Adam continued, "We'll be there at eight, have our starter and main course – then when it comes to the sweet, I'll order and you will bring Rachel a plate with one of those dome things on it. You'll whip it off and there will be the ring and a card saying, WILL YOU MARRY ME. It's going to be so romantic."

"What makes you think she'll want to marry an ugly brute like you?" Kenny teased.

"Enough!" Adam held his hand up. "I'm a bag of nerves as it is."

"Chill out man, it will be a dawdle. I could be a singing waiter, if you like."

"No way. You would empty the place in five minutes with your voice. Now be a pal and get me another pint."

On the big day, Kenny collected the ring and the card, promising to guard them with his life and to carry out Adam's instructions to the letter.

En route to work, Kenny dropped in to see his favourite librarian, Ann MacKay. Ann, fifty-something, with fifty-something hips and an infectious laugh, smiled as he approached.

"I'm dining in your place tonight," she told him.

"No! Really?"

"Yes my brother's home from Canada and he's taking me out for dinner."

"Well, first-class service for you," said Kenny, handing her his list. "Nothing but the best." And with a wink and a smile he was gone.

This little detour made him slightly late. Pietro was not amused.

"I tell you before, Kenneth. You get here on time or you no get here at all."

"Oh, keep your hair on, Pepe. I'm here now."

"You no call me Pepe – I tell you ten times already," he shouted, red-faced, and stormed off to the kitchen.

Lunchtime was chaotic, with orders coming quick and fast. Kenny tended to chat to customers, which didn't please his boss who prided himself on their speedy and efficient service.

Backing through the wrong door with a tray of dirty dishes, Kenny collided with Marco who was about to serve four bowls of minestrone.

"Stupido," roared Pietro. "This come off your wages, Kenneth – that teach you take care. Now clean up the mess and stay outa ma way."

The evening started badly. Truth to tell, Kenny was almost as nervous as Adam, though he would never have admitted it. He mixed up two orders, which caused an argument and to make matters worse, he overcharged a regular customer. Pietro had to use all his Latin charm to sort that one out.

There was worse to come. Kenny stretching over for a tray, somehow tipped a whole tub of chilli powder into a steaming pan of risotto. It was too much. Pietro turned puce.

"Get outa of ma kitchen and ma life," he cried. "I never wanna see you again."

Kenny wished he was dead. He slunk out, but on the way grabbed Marco's arm and pulled him into the foyer, explaining what he would have to do. At first, he was hesitant but finally agreed. The ring and card were handed over and Kenny headed for the pub.

At eight o'clock Adam arrived, escorting Rachel who looked stunning in a pale shift dress with blue embroidery which matched the satin ribbon tying back her soft fair hair. Her eyes shone as she took in the luxurious surroundings.

"It's gorgeous," she whispered, as she clutched Adam's hand.

"Table for Mackie," said Adam, looking anxiously for Kenny who was nowhere to be seen and it was Marco who showed them to a table set for two. He took their coats and gave them each a menu.

Ann and Alisdair McKay were already seated and she also expected to see Kenny, but turned her attention to the wine list.

Dinner fulfilled all Adam's hopes. Rachel was loving every bite of her chicken in white wine sauce with asparagus and tiny roast potatoes. He could barely taste his own food, but was certain that Kenny would not let him down. He beckoned the waiter to ask for the dessert menu. Rachel patted her tummy.

"Not sure I could eat any more, I'm quite full."

"Oh, but you must." He tried to keep the panic out of his voice. "They specialise in pudding here. Even if you only have ice-cream."

"Well, alright," she said, opening her menu.

On the other side of the room, Ann, flushed with pleasure and not a few glasses of white wine, was swithering over the dessert menu.

"Ah, sweets, I love them all," she sighed.as she tried to make a decision. "I think I'll go for zabaglione," she announced, but Alisdair refrained.

Deep in conversation with her brother, Ann barely noticed the arrival of her pudding till, with a flourish, the lid was removed to reveal a gigantic surprise.

"Oh, Marco!" she shrieked, when she managed to find her voice. "I will, I will." And she threw her ample bosom into his wildly protesting arms.

****

DRESS, SHOES AND CAKE

By Ashima Srivastava

Reema surfaced from under her duvet and stretched her arm to put the alarm on snooze. She wanted a few more minutes in the warm bed. Just then she felt Rahul's arms go round her and pull her towards him. Turning to him, Reema snuggled into his chest and smiled as hairs tickled her nose. She was lucky to have the warmth and comfort of those arms. Just then the alarm went off again. Wriggling out of Rahul's arms, Reema switched it off.

"Come back to me, Reem, it's barely six. Why are you so early? "

"I have a lot to do, Rahul, and you know I like everything done well before time," Reema replied, as she kissed him and got out of bed.

Reema made herself a fresh pot of coffee and looked over her menu. She would be meeting Rahul's parents for the first time tonight and she wanted everything to be perfect. They both had started working for Google at the same time and had soon become inseparable. Rahul's parents were arriving tonight from Bombay and they would be staying for a month.

"I think I should stay at mine while your parents are here Rahul," she had said when he first told her about their visit.

"Why Reema?" Rahul asked.

"They will want to spend time with you, Rahul, they don't want me around," she had replied.

"Reem, you are an integral part of my life now and they will come to love you as much as I do."

They had gone back and forth on where she would stay whilst his parents were here. In the end Rahul had convinced her to stay.

Reema had decided on an Italian meal and had chosen a bottle of wine for every course. She was going to make her signature chocolate cake for dessert. She was still sipping her coffee when Rahul joined her. They would leave soon to go to buy all the fresh ingredients for the big dinner. Rahul could see how tense Reema was and he tried to reassure her.

"Just be yourself and everything will be fine," he said.

She nodded with a smile on her lips that didn't quite reach her eyes.

As they walked towards Borough Market, Rahul gave her list a once over. They bought a variety of cheese from Jumi Cheese, fresh fruits and vegetables from Stark's, fish from the Oak and Smoke, fresh flowers from the Garden Gate and the wines from Bedales of Borough. Laden with tote bags they grabbed some bread from the Karaway bakery and headed back home. As they walked past a shop window, Rahul saw a lovely red and black dress and he insisted they go in. Humouring him, Reema agreed. On glancing at herself in the mirror she felt the dress had been stitched just for her.

"It fits perfectly," she thought, as she came out and twirled in front of Rahul, she heard him take in a sharp breath.

"You look gorgeous, Darling," Rahul said, unable to take his eyes off her.

Adding another tote bag to their already full arms they continued their walk back. As they passed Crispin Shoes Reema saw a pair of red and black heels which would go perfectly with the dress.

A quick try for size, an even quicker purchase, and back to the walk, determined not to look at another shop window. The dinner wasn't going to cook itself.

By the time they had unpacked and put the flowers in fresh water it was close to noon. Reema could feel the panic rising. Putting on old Hindi songs on Spotify, she headed to the kitchen.

Rahul followed her and between the two of them they had everything done in no time.

Reema just had the cake to bake now.

They didn't have to leave for the airport for another three hours. Rahul had checked and the flight was on time.

"Will you run me a hot bath, please?" Reema called out over the loud music from the kitchen as she started on the cake batter.

"Okay, Darling," Rahul said, getting up from the sofa. Heading to the bathroom Rahul started filling the bath. He added the Epsom salts, bath oils, rose petals, and lit the candles.

"I think I will join Reema in the bath," he thought to himself with sparkling eyes.

Just then Rahul got a call from his accountant who needed some more information on his tax returns and Rahul had to make a quick dash to the study.

A good fifteen minutes later when he got off the phone, he remembered the bath. Rushing into the bathroom he stopped short as he saw the water overflowing

Muttering to himself he tiptoed through the water to close the tap. How do I hide this from Reema he thought to himself? Any chance of a soak with her was now quickly going down the drain with the water.

On hearing Rahul's footsteps, without turning around Reema asked, "Is the bath ready? The cake has just gone into the oven for thirty minutes and I am ready for that soak"

Hugging her from behind and nuzzling into her neck, Rahul whispered, "It's a disaster, Darling."

Spinning around in his arms with panic in her eyes and worry in her voice, she said, "What's happened?"

"A bit of a flood in the bathroom, my love. You go and put your feet up while I sort it out," he replied.

Walking towards the bathroom in frustration and anger she told him she would do it, and that he should stay out of her way. Getting the mop out, she opened the window, blew out the candles and started mopping. Twenty-five minutes later she was still sorting the bathroom and didn't hear the kitchen alarm beep letting her know it was time to take the cake out.

Rahul heard it and took it out and put off the oven. The cake had risen beautifully and when he pressed it gently in the centre like he had seen Reema do. It felt springy. He put it on a cooling rack and went back to his study and shut the door.

Just as Reema finished mopping she remembered the cake. Dropping the mop, she ran to the kitchen expecting she was going to find a burnt cake and a smoky kitchen. What greeted her instead was a perfect chocolate cake on the cooling rack.

Reema made filter coffee and placing two cups on a tray went to the study. Entering, she said, "That was not a disaster, Darling. Thank you for saving the cake."

Rahul had more than made up for his earlier screw-up.

Much later that night, when the cake was being served, Rahul narrated the proceedings of the day, his mess up with the bath and then how he had redeemed himself with the cake.

Reaching across to hold his hand, Reema said, "You are my cake-saving knight."

The evening ended on a happy note with a lot of laughter. As they headed to bed, they agreed the two of them were a good team.

****

LOCKDOWN

By Anjana Sen

We brave it out and isolate.
Virtual meets to stave off doom.
We write and meet to heal ourselves
In this cosy room that's Zoom.

****

I WAS ANGRY BUT SAID NOTHING

By Walter Sneader

I was angry but said nothing. Not because a billion or more dollars had been destroyed. No. It was the seven years of intense dedication and hard work that had disappeared in a fraction of a second. We should never have allowed the Americans to launch our satellite. We could have done it ourselves if the government had not been so penny pinching. Sure, it would have cost more. Perhaps another two hundred million pounds. But now we had lost everything.

After a few stunned seconds, I requested to be put through to Commander Jackson in Cape Kennedy. I recognised his familiar drawl.

"Hi, Richard. Looks like something went wrong."

I gasped at his glib comment. "What happened?" I asked. "We've worked our asses off for years to get the satellite finished. And your guys have destroyed it."

My anger had little impact. He simply continued with little emotion.

"I've got my chief engineer already on to it. He'll get to the bottom of it pretty damn quick. I know you guys must be upset, but these things do happen. It's unfortunate it was your satellite that bit the dust."

"Unfortunate! That's a bit of an understatement," I shouted. "Good grief. Incompetence is more like it. I'll see that those responsible pay for this. If it includes you, so be it."

There was no reply. I moved to the back of the room to find out what was causing the shouting over there. As I drew near, I could see our press officer was having a blazing row with three or four reporters.

"I'm trying to tell you that they don't know either, It only happened a few minutes ago. I'll tell you as soon as I have something"

Poor John. There would be no peace until they got a story from him. Then I thought of what lay ahead for myself. Doubtless there would be a call from the Secretary of State in a few minutes, I had to prepare myself for the worst.

The phone rang. I was right. It was Jeremy Caruthers.

"I say, old boy, the Yanks have really messed up this time. Have you any idea what went wrong?"

"No sir. Jackson has promised to call me as soon as he finds out. Until then, there's nothing I can tell you. But you will get a roasting from parliament, no doubt."

"If that's your way of digging at me for not letting our boys take care of the launch, I would advise you to keep your bloody moth shut!"

I heard the receiver being slammed down. I knew it was time for me to get out of there.

After a sleepless night I was awoken by the phone ringing. It was Jackson.

"OK. I've got our preliminary findings. It looks like a computer fault."

"What! Did somebody forget to plug it in?"

"Calm down. There's nearly two hundred thousand lines of code in the lift off program. One of them has an error, but there's something very suspicious. The guy who wrote that bit swears it wasn't present in the version he prepared. And he has produced his own copy. It supports what he said. The security people are on to this. They are discussing it with Langley."

I thought your guys had the tightest security possible. Only the Russians or Chinese would have been capable of getting past it."

"That's exactly what our people are saying. They think Putin is behind it. His revenge for our kicking out forty of his spies last month."

"Makes sense." I paused for a few moments. "Can I tell the press? They're at our heels for information."

"It's the same here," he replied. T think we will need to keep this hush hush for the time being. We are putting out a story about a timing error causing pre-ignition and a consequent explosion."

"OK. That's what I'll tell them, too. But you'll need to keep me in the picture."

"Don't worry. I will. Promise."

Thankfully the story blew over in a couple of days. There were a few questions to Caruthers in parliament. The Prime Minister saved his skin, though I don't think he'll survive the next Cabinet reshuffle. And good riddance.

My story would have ended there were it not for an expose in the Sunday Times.

"U S cover up over British Satellite Destruction", read the headline. And in the following paragraphs it revealed that Russian hackers had managed to penetrate American security. They were able to corrupt the computer code for the launch of the British Satellite. Full details were given about how this had been done complete with detailed diagrams.

When I walked into my office later that morning Jeremy Caruthers was sitting waiting for me.

"Have you seen it?" he asked, menacingly.

"Yes. Pretty awful."

"Thank heavens it didn't happen at our end. The PM wanted to know if you had any inkling of this. Did you?"

"Jackson mentioned a rumour to that effect. But, as far as I know it was never confirmed."

"Why didn't you report that to me?"

"It was only a rumour, sir."

"Right. You're for the chop!"

With that, I stormed out. Half an hour later my phone rang again.

"Prime Minister here. Caruthers has just told me that you knew about the Russian involvement. Yet you never told us. That's appalling. There is no way you can be trusted anymore. Please leave your office immediately. There is a security officer standing at your door. Do not return. And remember that you have signed the Official Secrets Act. If you say anything about this to anyone, you will be arrested. Goodbye."

That was it. I had been fired. And I was bound to silence.

"Don't worry," a reassuring voice responded. "We will see that no harm comes to you. Mr Putin himself will ensure that you are properly rewarded for the help you have given us. Without your confirmation, we couldn't be certain that we had succeeded in altering the computer code. We will now be able to make extensive use of that technique. The Americans will never know what hit them."

****

WAS IT A GHOST?

By Jim Morrison.

Rab White put his pint on the table and sat down. His Jack Russel companion, Brad, jumped on to his lap. He looked about the bar. He had been coming to the Golden Plover every day, except for when he was on holiday, for the last twenty-five years. Brad had been with him for sixteen of them. Rab looked down at his dog.

"Ach," he thought, "We're both getting on. It takes us twice as long to get here as it used to." He liked the feel of the pub. It still had a slightly old-fashioned look and atmosphere. "A typical Glasgow howf," he thought.

He knew most of the regulars, of course. Whereas he used to stand at the bar and enjoy the crack, he was now happy to sit and watch. Benny, the barman, had been pulling pints for at least twenty years. And there was Denise. \she was another regular of long-standing. Rab was content. This was a second home to him. A place where he felt comfortable.

"Comfortable, that's how I feel here. A good way to describe it," he thought, then, looking round, "That's funny, I don't remember that door ever being there."

The door in question was on the wall two or three yards in front of him. It was painted to match the rest of the pub with a large glass panel in the top half which was etched with a leafy floral pattern around the edge. The door was opened by a friendly looking man who beckoned to Rab. Intrigued, he stood up and went over.

"Come in," said the man. "I've been waiting for you."
Rab went into the adjoining room. "Why?" he asked.
"It's time," the stranger replied, nodding towards the door.

Rab stared through the glass. He saw himself sitting at the table. Well, more slumped as if he was asleep. He looked at his companion who smiled slightly and nodded.

"Oh, I get it. I'm ..." he hesitated.

"Aye, it's time."

As the old man looked back at himself a sudden sad thought crossed his mind.

"My dog, Brad," he said. "He's old like me. He wouldn't fit with anyone else. Could I take him with me?"

The man thought for a minute and then smiled. "Aye, you can have him. Call him."

"Thanks man," said Rab. "Here, boy," he called.

In the pub the customers were startled to hear Brad barking. That was something he never did. Someone looked over, "Here, I don't think auld Rab looks so good."

One of the men went to speak to Rab. "Benny, you better phone for an ambulance. I think he's deid."

As Benny made the telephone call the customers gathered round the table.

Someone said, "Would you look at that? I think the dog has gone as well."

Something made Denise look up. There was Rab standing near the wall and he had Brad in his arms. It was just for a second and then he was gone. She was stunned.

Was it a ghost she had seen? Denise thought about it for a minute. She said nothing to anyone, but for the rest of life she kept in her mind the wonderful picture of the old man standing there with his pet in his arms and the look of pure devotion with which the dog was looking at his friend.

****

BABY BLUES

By Nada Mooney

I'm carrying this box carefully because it's got a little rabbit in it. I got it from my friend Michelle. I hope they let me keep it- I've always wanted one.

When I asked my mum for a bunny, she said no, I was getting something much better, a wee brother or sister to play with.

I waited and waited, but nobody came. Mum just got very fat and then one day she said she had to go to the hospital and I was sent to Granny and Grandpa's.

I hate my Granny. She smokes cigarettes and talks on the phone all day. Grandpa is even worse. He drinks something he calls medicine and if he has a lot he sometimes falls down. There are no toys in their house and they don't even have a garden.

When they let me go home, Mummy was back, but she had this horrid baby with her.

It just sleeps and cries- it can't even talk. And it's a boy, I wanted a sister.

So this morning, while my mum was having a rest, and the baby was in its pram, I took it to Michelle's and changed it for a rabbit. She said her mum's got so many babies, she wouldn't notice another one.

I think they'll be quite pleased. Rabbits never cry and they don't need nappies either. Oh, here's mum coming now. I wonder why she's running?

****

MIRROR IMAGE

By Anjana Sen

I got a fright, I must confess
As I brushed my teeth this morning.
There you were in the mirror.
Ma, you popped up without warning.
My greys have merged with yours I see,
My eyes flash the same way, too.
The years have smudged my sharp jawline
And turned me into you.
Folk said how much I looked like you.
I never saw it till just now.
And yet, here I am, in the mirror
With your chin, your smile your brow.
It's not just the way we look,
I speak like you these days.
The funny annoying things you said
Have become a part of my own ways.
Images of you were a challenge for me.
I worried so about the grief,
But I've found you here, in my mirror
And am filled with wild relief.
Relieved to have you by my side.
And, also, one more thought.
If I have turned into you, Ma,
My daughter will soon be me, will she not?

****

INTRODUCING THE WRITERS

ANN MORRISON

Ann joined Eastwood Writers fourteen years ago as a complete novice and now has the pleasure of serving as President for the second time. She describes Eastwood as a very friendly club, focused on supporting each other, both in writing and by continuing to meet via Zoom every week throughout the current crisis. Her thanks go to those with the technical knowledge who set up the system and helped those of us who were not so able to use it. Eastwood Writers are affiliated to the Scottish Association of Writers and every year are represented at their Annual Conference and members have been successful in their competitions. She attributes this Anthology to Pamela Duncan and says it is thanks to her we are able to share our work with you. As President of the club, Ann brings a calm, sensible influence to our very lively and diverse membership.

WALTER SNEADER

Walter joined Eastwood Writers over six years ago. Prior to retirement he was the Head of the School of Pharmacy at the University of Strathclyde. He has written four books, mainly about the history of drug discovery. The most recent of these was published in 2005 and is still in print after selling thousands of copies. He admits he now prefer writing fiction. A wizard of technology, Walter sets up our lockdown meetings on Zoom.

ANJANA SEN

An army brat, Anjana grew up all over India, and later followed her husband around the world before settling down in Glasgow in the year 2000. She has always loved everything to do with words and discovered Eastwood Writers by default and started writing with them to escape the empty nest blues. Now, she is hooked on to writing, poetry mostly, and assists the club with secretarial duties. Her lovely smile lifts everyone's spirits each session.

PAMELA DUNCAN

Pamela, a former local reporter, is a founder member of the club. She has won numerous trophies for writing, including the Scottish Association of Writers' Scholarship and has received forty award certificates covering most creative writing genres. Four of her novels have been published along with nearly 200 poems. Some of the latter have been broadcast on radio networks She has adjudicated for the SAW, Falkirk Writers and Ottakars/Faber Competitions. She served for 13 years as Writing Representative for East Renfrewshire on it's Arts Development Forum and co-organised Glasgow's popular WORDS & MUSIC Performance Club for 22 years. Pamela was also on the Management Committee of Ayr Club WRITABILITY. One of her plays was performed at Edinburgh's Workshop Theatre She has twice been President of Eastwood Writers.

EMILY M CLARK

Was still working when she joined Greenock Writers and was encouraged by winning their cup for a children's story. When she moved to Netherlee, she thought she was finished with writing until she heard of the Eastwood Writers. Emily has been a member now for twenty years, receiving the constructive criticism necessary to move writing to a higher level. She has contributed greatly to the group.

DONALD MONTGOMERY

Donald joined Eastwood Writers in 2007 and has since won several writing competitions. Already a published author, a collection of feel-good stories set in an affluent retirement complex, *Welcome to Somerville Grange*, will be published soon by *Next Chapter*. Donald is noted for having a keen sense of observation and for his unique humour.

NADA MOONEY

Nada is a long-standing member of Eastwood Writers. There is a defined skill in producing a short story in a concise format and she has mastered this. Several of her flash fiction stories are featured in our anthology along with some poems.

JOYCE MCKENDRY

Joyce came across Eastwood Writers through an advert in a local paper and has been a member for ten years. An avid reader, mainly Penny Vincenzi and Jody Picoult, her favourite poet is Pam Ayres. She was a legal secretary for over forty years and is married to Gerry and has a son, Gary. Joyce served the club as secretary for several years and her stories never fail to appeal.

GERRY MCKENDRY

Gerry spent most of his working life in Photographic Retail. His lifelong interest, however, is in magic. He has always written poems and short stories for his own amusement and has combined the two interests by writing poems for the world's leading magicians. Gerry is known as the *'Poet Laureate of Magic'* and is a lifetime Honorary Vice President of the Scottish Conjurers. He has a very keen wit and entertains the members with a few tricks from time to time. He is married to Eastwood member Joyce.

MYRNA SNEADER

Myrna joined Eastwood Writers during the Coronaviral lockdown. Prior to retiring, she was Teacher in Charge of a nursery school for most of her career. Her enjoyment of writing began at school and has now been rekindled. She draws on her own memories to contribute stories and articles to our weekly meetings and is married to Walter.

KATE RICHARD

Was born and educated in Edinburgh and had a career as an academic librarian. Having moved to Glasgow, she attended adult education classes in creative writing in the nineties where she wrote poetry and short stories. After working with a charity, she started writing again when she joined Eastwood Writers and has proved a welcome addition to the membership.

ALISTAIR MACLELLAN

Has always enjoyed writing and worked for a short time in broadcasting for the BBC. Developing fictional characters and plots was something he had never done until he became a member of Eastwood Writers two years ago. Both the club and this genre of writing have opened up a whole new world for him which he thoroughly delights in and embraces. Alistair is an inspirational figure in the group.

JIM MORRISON

Jim describes himself as a new member of Eastwood Writers and says he was talked into joining by his wife, Ann. This has enabled him to learn about writing from people with lots of experience in different genres. In his previous life, he was a police officer and in those days his writing consisted of long-winded police reports. Now he enjoys the challenge of Eastwood's varied syllabus and the encouragement of his new friends.

ASHIMA SRIVASTAVA

Living in the beautiful and vibrant city of Glasgow, Ashima joined Eastwood Writers early in 2020. She has always enjoyed writing and is thankful to everyone for the encouragement, advice and support sha has received. Her husband and daughters have been an inspiration through their love and belief in her. Ashima has the potential to go far with her writing. She hopes you have enjoyed both of her stories.

****

A BRIEF HISTORY OF EASTWOOD WRITERS

Eastwood Writers was founded in 1985 when a class led by the late Clarkston author, Pat Gerber, concluded. Having benefitted from two years' tuition, the class, consisting of around twenty enthusiastic members, was keen to continue writing. The local district council supported the club with grants until it became established. Eastwood Writers affiliated with the Scottish Association of Writers and has featured regularly on the Association's Prize Lists at their Annual Conferences.

The club is made up of both experienced and new writers. Support, encouragement and constructive criticism are offered and the set syllabus is designed to cover all genres of Creative Writing. Following the syllabus is not compulsory and those working on a project such as a novel are free to present it for comment. Over the years, the group has become a relaxed and happy haven for what is a rewarding hobby. A fair proportion of the membership has seen work published.

Today. Eastwood Writers has a membership of fourteen and continues to flourish. The group acknowledges the part Woodfarm High School, Thornliebank, has played in hosting the weekly meetings for many years until the Covid-19 pandemic forced lockdown. A resilient group, Eastwood immediately turned to Zoom and, courtesy of the internet, weekly sessions have continued. Zoom proved so popular that even the normal summer recess was abandoned.

For inclusion in this anthology members submitted work of their own choice. Only the minimum of editing has taken place so that the individual voices of writers have been preserved.

Our hope is that you enjoy reading our work and, though doors may be closed, ours are always open to welcome new members.

****

REMEMBER, FOR EVERY BOOK SOLD £1 IS DONATED TO MACMILLAN CANCER CARE

Printed in Great Britain
by Amazon

55866434R00071